Other Books by Nicholas Bruner

The Last Days of Atlantis series
Mother Ink (Book 1)
Brother Flute (Book 2)
Daughter Cloud (Book 3)

The Heroes of Atlantis series
Sister Honey (Book 1) (coming Fall 2024)

Hard Santa Case Files
O Trolly Night (Book 1)

Other Books
The Ballad of Dani and Eli
A Far Ocean's Tale and Other Stories
Jesus Bugs
The Love Machine
Roll dem Bones

All books available at Amazon
(amazon.com/author/nicholasbruner)

Sign up for my mailing list and receive ***Orphan Stone***, the free prequel to the Last Days of Atlantis trilogy!
https://www.subscribepage.com/s8d7d6

O Trolly Night
© 2023 Nicholas Bruner

ALL RIGHTS RESERVED. No part of this work may be reproduced or transmitted in any form or by any means, electronic or mechanical, including photocopying and recording, or by any information storage or retrieval system without the proper written permission of the appropriate copyright holder listed below, unless such copying is expressly permitted by federal and international copyright law.

ISBN 979-8-9896396-0-1

Cover design by Moorbooks Design

*Now all around the world
the fact is widely known
the North Pole or thereabouts
is where Santa makes his home.*

*And there's no one who works harder
than Santa and his elves
making toys and games for children
to put upon their shelves.*

*For months of every year
they slog and slave and sweat
so all deserving youngsters
will have something special they can get.*

*But what you might not realize
is that when Christmastime is done.
Santa and his missus
like to have themselves some fun.*

*Surely you don't begrudge
Saint Nick his share of enjoyment?
While he and Mrs. Claus
take a break from their employment?*

*For them, January, February, and March,
is that magic time of year
when they can kick back, relax,
and quaff a couple beers.*

*Yes, they like to take their ease,
and put aside their hurries.
They spend a season perhaps in Belize
(or the Florida Keys),
to forget all about their worries.*

*Yet, as we shall see, for Santa Claus
there's always trouble brewing.
But for right now, let's just check in
and see what it is they're doing....*

Chapter One

Nick took a sip of his piña colada through a straw and sighed with contentment. The icy sweet-tart drink washed cold down his throat, with more than a hint of alcohol aftertaste. A gentle warm breeze blew under the tails of his Hawaiian shirt, up his back, and under his long white beard. Waves crashed endlessly against the beach, with the occasional distant happy shouts of kids splashing each other or running through the surf. The easy shade under the cabana contrasted with the hard bright light of the Miami Beach sun outside.

A low whistle and a shout of "¡Ay, mamacita!" from somewhere down the boardwalk caught Nick's ear. He turned his head and spied what was causing the ruckus: a woman with waist-length braids of reddish-brown hair, sporting a red and green-striped string bikini and Ray-Ban sunglasses, strolled nonchalantly along the pathway. The dappled shadows of the palm trees along the boardwalk played across her browned skin, and men and women alike stopped walking or biking and turned just to gaze at her as she walked by. Her stomach was taut and toned, her legs long and tawny as a gazelle's, her bikini top well-filled and with the barest hint of nipple visible though the silken fabric.

Hot damn, the old girl's still got it, Nick thought, turning back to his drink with a faint smile. He nodded at the woman as she ducked under the fringe of the cabana.

"You seem to be drawing some attention with your outfit, Anya."

"Am I?" Anya replied, taking the stool next to his. "I hadn't noticed."

The bartender finished serving the customers at the other end of the bar and came down to see to his new arrival. "Good afternoon, Mrs. Kringle. Can I get you something?"

"I'll have what he's having." Anya pointed at Nick's glass.

"Very good, ma'am. One piña colada coming right up."

He stepped away to mix the ingredients. Nick raised an eyebrow. "I thought you were going shopping. Didn't you find anything?"

"Of course I did," Anya said. "I didn't want to have to lug all those bags around all day. I had it all sent to the hotel."

"Bags?" Nick said. "I hope you left something for the other customers."

"I didn't buy too much. A couple sundresses, another swimsuit. Oh, and a few pairs of shoes."

"A few pairs? How many?"

"Not too many," Anya said.

"How. Many. Pairs." Nick growled.

"...not *too* many." The bartender turned on the blender and Anya leaned over and whispered in Nick's ear. "Oh, and I got something to wear tonight, as well. For later on. A special gift, just for you." She grinned wickedly. "But you'll have to unwrap it yourself."

Nick had encircled his big rough hand around his

drink and the glass shattered. The bartender rushed over with a towel. "Is everything okay here, Mr. Kringle?"

"S-sorry about that," Nick stammered. "I must have slammed the glass down a little too hard."

Anya Kringle settled back on her stool and smirked at her husband while the bartender wiped up the spill. "Not a problem at all. Let me get you another one, sir."

"You know, I was thinking about switching to wine anyway," Nick said. Before he could continue, a ring tone went off, playing "O Christmas Tree." Nick pulled his phone out from the back pocket of his swimtrunks and mouthed "the elves" at Anya, with a roll of his eyes. "Hello?"

The bartender slid Anya's drink to her and she brought it to her lips while Nick talked. The responding voice on the other end of the line was almost comically high-pitched, though only Nick's end of the conversation could be made out. "Uh huh... the new workshop, are you serious? You're shittin' me, right? No...right. I can be up there tonight... No, I don't need the whole team. Just send down a couple. Donner and Blitzen... Yeah, good idea. Set up a couple elves to watch it, make sure he doesn't come back. But if he shows up and starts any trouble, don't try to stop him. Just wait for me to get there...Yeah, see you then." He hit the end call button and tucked the phone back in his pocket.

Anya set her drink down with an angry clink. "Nick, I fucking know that call wasn't you agreeing to leave to go deal with business."

"It's just for tonight, baby," Nick said.

Anya shot him a look. "It's February, Nick. Part of

our three months off."

Nick put his hand on top of Anya's but she withdrew it. "Listen, baby. I'll fly out at midnight, and be back by morning. It's a break-in at the new workshop, no big deal. Probably one of the Yule Lads. You'll hardly notice I'm gone."

"Yeah, I've heard that before," Anya said. "You do remember Friday's my birthday, right? With my big party?"

"Don't worry, baby. That's three days away." Nick leaned over and kissed Anya on the cheek. "I'll be back by then, I promise. I wouldn't miss your three hundred-fiftieth for all the snow in Nome."

"You really promise?" Anya pouted her lips.

"I really do. And you know you don't look a day over three hundred." Nick gave her a wink and checked his Blancpain Air Command watch. "Hey, we need to head back and change soon. Don't we have reservations at Macchialina tonight?"

"At seven," Anya said. "That's two-and-a-half hours from now."

"Right." Nick leaned over and spoke in a low tone. "And if that outfit you were talking about is as sexy as I'm imagining, two-and-a-half hours might not be enough time for what I have planned. So finish your drink, and let's head back."

"Nuh uh." Anya shook her head. "You don't get to see it unless you keep your promise. If you're back by Friday for my party at seven, I put it on for you. Not before then."

Nick exhaled hard through his nose. "Shit, baby.

You've got to let me see you in it. I've got a hard-on right now just thinking about it."

"You heard me," Anya said. "You have three days. You're back by Friday at seven, you get the reward. And Nick, one more thing."

"What's that, baby?"

"If you're *not* back by Friday, you're going on my naughty list. And you know what that means." Nick was about to interject something but Anya put a perfectly manicured index finger to his lips. "No nookie until *I* decide to take you off the list."

* * *

The troll king spun his lucky penguin femur through the green-furred fingers of one hand, the digits long and slender as French green beans. With his other hand, he stirred the steaming liquid in a big, round iron cauldron over a bed of coals with a long wooden rod. From time to time, he used the flattened end of the rod to clear away the stinking, pea-green foam from the liquid's surface and peered into its black depths.

The door opened and a lissome woman with pallid skin, ice blue eyes, and a long blonde braid poked her head in. She wore a filmy blue dress spangled with embroidered ice crystals. "Oh, here you are, in this weird room," she said. "Have you seen Roscoe?"

"Er, no. I'm sure he's around somewhere. But Inga, my love, you are just who I wanted to see," the troll king said in his sniveling voice. "Come in, come in."

The corner of Inga's mouth turned down. "Do I have

to? It's hot as a Finnish sauna in here."

"Ah, yes, the temperature set too high for the ice queen, is it? No matter, this won't take long. I only want you to come see my latest project."

Inga stepped a few paces into the room.

"Closer, my dear. You have to look into the broth to see."

"Whatever you're cooking stinks like you're boiling elk shit," Inga said. "I hope to hell this isn't our soup course tonight."

"Of course not. And the aroma comes from very rare and particular herbs I've picked from the Forbyr Forest."

"Remind me not to put you in charge of making the potpourri this year," Inga said. "Why didn't you pick something that smelled better?"

"Because these are the herbs necessary for the spell to work." The troll king cleared the liquid's surface with his rod. "Never mind the smell. Look in and tell me what you see."

Inga bent at her waist and gazed into the broth. As she stared, the liquid clarified and she could make out two figures seated at a table in an elegant restaurant. An auburn-haired woman dressed in a strapless magenta dress spun spaghetti onto a spoon, while her companion, a stout, white-bearded man in a red tuxedo jacket, brought a huge meatball to his lips. "Why, it's Anya and Nick!" She sighed wistfully. "It's been so long since I've gotten to see them. Or *any*body. Is this taking place now?"

"At this very moment, my dear. You see, the husband

of your old college roommate is about to fall into a trap I've set."

Inga's expression changed to a sneer. "Good. Serves her right. The little bitch always did get everything she wanted." But then her eyes narrowed at her husband. "And what are you planning with Anya after Nick's gone? I suppose you think you'll have a shot with her then."

The troll king raised his hands in protest. "No, you misunderstand me! The woman has nothing to do with the plot."

"Are you sure." Inga's voice indicated it was more of a threat than a question.

"Of course I'm sure, my dear. This is a diabolical plan of the first order, something only my fiendish mind could have conceived. First, I've located Old Saint Nick's newest workshop, using means that would astound you, if I could even explain it in a way you were capable of comprehending. Second, I've taken what's most precious in his workshop without his even knowing, an intellectual coup of immense proportions. And third, even if the old dolt somehow figures out where it's gone, I've laid out a special surprise for his arrival here. A surprise only I could devise that will take Saint Nick out of the picture, permanently."

Inga's attention had drifted during the troll king's monologue and her eyes glazed. The troll king rapped the penguin femur against the wooden stick, and Inga snapped back. "Oh," she said. "Well, what's all that have to do with me?"

"My dear, it has everything to do with you. After all, don't you always complain how dank it is here? And how

I never take you anywhere?"

"Well, yeah," Inga admitted. "This castle's terrible. And two hundred years of marriage, with no vacation."

"I cannot help my situation, my dear, as I've explained many times."

"Yes, yes, the curse of the people of Howburg." Inga sighed. "And just to rub it in, Inga's forever sending me postcards from whatever exotic spot she and Nick are visiting. I wish I could trade places with her right fucking now."

"They're in Miami," the troll king noted dryly. "I didn't think you would care to visit that place."

"Well, I guess Miami would be pretty warm for me, but Vail would be nice. Or the Alps. Couldn't we go skiing sometime?"

"Soon, my dear," the troll king said. "You see, after the successful execution of my plan, we'll be able to go wherever you want, for we'll have our own supply of elf dust. And with the elf dust, even the curse that binds me to the Troll Kingdom won't be able to stop me from leaving. But best of all, without his supply, Saint Nick won't be able to make his reindeer fly. Christmas will be ruined!"

"Truly?" Inga said. "We'll be able to travel anywhere?"

"Anywhere you like," the troll king said. "Does that please you?"

"I'll believe it when I see it," Inga said. She walked to the door. "I have to go look for Roscoe."

"You know, I think he said he planned to camp overnight in the forest. I wouldn't bother searching for him. "The troll king cleared his throat. "Er, Inga, my love. Before you go."

Inga sighed. "Yes, what is it, Groschen?"

The troll king tapped the tips of his long fingers together. "I wonder if tonight, you might be willing to stop by my sleeping chamber. Or, I could stop by yours. And we could...you know." He raised his bushy green eyebrows.

"Keep dreaming, troll boy." Inga slammed the door behind her.

***

At 386 feet, the roof of the Setai Hotel at midnight was far chillier than the Miami Beach boardwalk in the afternoon. Still, Nick showed no signs of being bothered by the temperature or the gusts of wind. He hadn't even changed out of his Hawaiian shirt. He stood by the railing and regarded the twinkling Miami skyline to the west. For years, they had struggled with finding a hotel in Miami that didn't have a rooftop pool or party area, so that Nick could make a quick getaway when necessary. Finally, they'd given up and simply begun booking the Setai's penthouse suite when they were in town.

After several minutes, he checked his watch. *12:06. I can't believe those bastards.*

Just then, a sledge pulled by two reindeer silhouetted across the Florida moon. Almost faster than the eye could track, the sledge descended and landed next to the pool. The reindeer took little reverse steps to slow their speed and the sledge's runners scraped against the concrete deck. It was one of the compact, sporty models, not the full-sized luxury sleigh reserved for ceremonial occasions.

"Took you two fucking long enough," Nick scolded. One of the reindeer snorted in response, the other emitted a low grunt. "Okay, okay, watch your language."

He checked under the seat of the sledge and pulled out a five-foot warhammer, hefting it in one hand. The fifteen-pound head, made of forged lead, consisted of a square face on one side, and on the other, a wickedly curved spike ending in the shape of an antler. Its thick haft was carved from white beech wood, worn smooth from centuries of use.

"Good, Hordi didn't forget the Ulvehammer." Nick gave the weapon a quick, two-handed practice swing and placed it carefully back under the seat, just in case. He took one look back at Anya through the skylight, sleeping soundly under the hotel's high threadcount sheets, her long hair spread like a Japanese fan across the comforter. She shifted and the blanket threatened to uncover one perfect breast, but she pulled the covers back up to her chin.

Nick took his place on the seat and picked up the reins in one hand. From his pocket, he pulled out a handful of a grainy substance that most observers would have taken for soft sand from Miami Beach's white shoreline. But when he tossed it over the reindeer, it sparkled most peculiarly. *Good old elf dust*, he thought. Giving the reins a shake, he cried, "On Donner, on Blitzen! To Nytt Verksted!"

Chapter Two

Nick steered the sledge low over the hilly tundra, covered with white except where rock formations poked through the snow blanket. The sky was clear and starry, and the crisp air was cracking cold. With a quick flick of the reins, Nick signalled the reindeer to curve, and they veered sharply between two escarpments that created a canyon between them. He brought the sledge in hot, roaring through the overhanging pebbled rock walls to either side, and pulling the vehicle up next to a low-slung cabin, a quarter-mile long, and built in the shadow of the rocks.

"Whoa!" he cried, and Donner and Blitzen skidded to a stop, sending up a shower of powdery snow.

Nick alit on the level, snow-covered trail leading to the cabin's double front doors. Before he reached the entrance, one of the doors opened and an elf emerged, about five feet tall with long, pointed ears, combed-back dark hair, and a perfectly trimmed moustache and goatee. He was dressed smartly in a crisp green caftan under a black, waist-length coat and shod with gleaming black boots, round glasses halfway down his nose, and checking an iPad as he strode briskly.

"Hrodi, what's the word?" Nick called out.

Hrodi raised his eyes from the iPad and glanced Nick up and down over his glasses, taking in Nick's swim trunks, Hawaiian shirt, and flip-flops. He arched a black bushy eyebrow and spoke in his high, nasal voice. "You sure you don't want me to get you something more appropriate to wear first, Boss?"

"I'm good. It can't be more than, what, ten below?" Nick said.

"Fourteen below Fahrenheit, twenty-five Celsius," Hrodi replied. "Do you want the latest production report, or should we go straight to the break-in site?"

"Let's head to the site," Nick said, already starting toward the door. "You said it was one of the rear windows near the lab?"

"Exactly so," Hrodi said, extending his stride to keep up with the much larger man. He snapped his fingers and instantly half a dozen elves in green overalls emerged from the building and began unharnessing the reindeer. "I knew you'd want to inspect everything closely, so I ordered the area to remain undisturbed."

"Very good," Nick said. They passed through the double doors and into the workshop itself. If the place had looked rustic, even cozy from the outside, inside it was all gleaming surfaces and ultra-modern equipment. Hundreds of elves, dressed in green, red, or blue overalls, busied themselves with setting up the conveyer belts of assembly lines and positioning plastic molding machines or multi-axis laser cutters, while others carried boxes of raw plastic beads, wooden dowels, metal screws, batteries, or microchips and arrayed them neatly in rows. Line managers, dressed similarly to Hrodi, watched over the workers or made notes on iPads, occasionally pointing out to workers how to better arrange something.

"How's the production line for the Pretty Kitty Ultimate Cook-at-Home Set®?" Nick asked.

"Coming along nicely," Hrodi said. "I think we should be able to get five thousand units a week out of it."

Nick shook his head. "Not enough. That item's going to be hot shit this year. It'll be moving like flapjacks at a lumberjack convention."

"We could set up dual lines and double the output," Hrodi suggested. "But we'd have to cut back on the Real Bumpin' Monster Crash Race Car Track®."

"Yeah, do that," Nick said. "The boys aren't into car racers much anymore. Too many fuckin' video games. We got stuck with a shitload of last year's model."

"Got it, Boss." Hrodi scrolled through a screen on his iPad and typed in a couple notes as they walked. "Double the Pretty Kitty sets." He glanced up. "Ah, here we are."

They'd crossed the workshop floor and entered a laboratory where elves wearing white coats and protective goggles soldered metal pieces with blowtorches or mixed ingredients in beakers. Hrodi led Nick to a window at the back that had been covered with cardboard. There was shattered glass and rock debris spilled across the floor and yellow tape strung across orange cones blocked off the area. At a nod from Hrodi, two elves standing guard moved back.

Nick stepped over the yellow tape and squatted, picking up rock and glass shards, blowing away the gray-white rock dust, and examining them in the light. "When did this happen?"

"We found it after the six o'clock wake-up bell this morning, so it must have been sometime overnight."

"The nightwatch didn't hear anything?"

"We have them stationed at the front door," Hrodi said. "I guess the noise was too far away to carry."

"Wait a minute." Nick looked up. "You called me at four-thirty this afternoon. Why didn't you contact me as soon as you discovered it?"

"That's just after lunch, local time, Boss," Hrodi pointed out.

"Still, you let hours pass. When were you going to let me know?"

Hrodi shrugged. "It looked like some rocks fell from the escarpment. Rockfall's hardly a rarity, and no cause for concern. Why bother you about it when you're on vacation? So I ordered a new window and we followed the typical isolation procedure whenever there's an incident. I was simply going to write it up in the daily report, until"—he pointed underneath a nearby industrial freezer inside the taped-off area—"we noticed that."

Nick glanced under the freezer. "Huh." He reached under and pulled out an oversized metal spoon, the handle slightly bent, the bowl encrusted with dried pink food remains. Nick gave it a sniff. "Yogurt. Raspberry, I think."
Hrodi nodded. "Right. That's when we realized it was more serious. A spoon means it must have been Skyrgámur, the yogurt gobbler. At that point, I called you right away."

"If it was Skyrgámur, he broke into the kitchen then, as well," Nick pushed himself to his feet. "Let's go take a look."

"That's the thing, Boss," Hrodi said. "There's nothing missing in the kitchen, or even anything that looks like it's been touched. Hell, there weren't even any muddy bootprints to mop up."

Nick stroked his beard. "That *is* odd. There should have been one hell of a mess waiting for you there when you woke up."

"Maybe an elf got up in the middle of the night to take a piss, and scared him off?" Hrodi said.

"I don't think so," Nick said. "The Yule Lads may be skittish, but they're also tenacious. If he broke in, he's not leaving until he finds the food. But besides that, we just moved. This is the workshop's first year of operation. How did he already know the place was even here?"

Hrodi only shook his head.

"Something's not right here," Nick said. "Have you checked outside yet?"

"Not yet, Boss. But remember, until this afternoon, we didn't think there was anything suspicious."

"Got it. You're not in trouble, by the way. You handled it just the way you should have."

Hrodi pushed his glasses partway up the bridge of his nose. "Thanks, Boss."

"Al-fuckin'-righty, then. Let's go see what we have out there."

Outside, the cold air was still and the moon shone directly overhead, brightly illuminating the canyon. A gap of about fifty yards lay between the log-hewn walls of the workshop building and the steep, pebbled face of the escarpment, which jutted straight up two hundred feet. The ground was covered with packed snow, with the area outside the broken window littered with a spread of fallen rock, itself partially covered with a thick dusting of new-fallen snow.

"Damn it," Nick said as he surveyed the scene.

"What's wrong?" Hrodi asked.

"The fresh snow," Nick answered. "I was hoping to look for Skyrgámur's tracks. See how he got here, and if there was a second set showing where he went after leaving."

"He must have climbed down the cliff face, though," Hrodi said. "Surely that's what caused the rockfall. Maybe it even broke the window unintentionally, but he took advantage of it. Then I figure he simply got spooked by something."

"Hmm." Nick walked to the cliff face and stared up for a long time, scanning the rock. "I wonder if that's...."

"Do you see something?" Hrodi asked, following.

Without another word, Nick unbuttoned and threw off his Hawaiian shirt, kicked off his flipflops, found a handhold in the wall, and began climbing. His ample belly rubbed against the rock, his broad shoulder and back muscles flexed, and his calves worked like writhing serpents as he inserted his toes into crevices and pushed off of jutting rocks.

"Boss, be careful! If Skyrgámur caused a rockfall when he climbed, think about how much more than him you weigh!"

Nick grunted but otherwise ignored Hrodi's exhortations and continued to make his way up. Despite the Arctic air, his body developed a sheen of perspiration and beads of sweat ran down his temples and into his beard. About fifty feet up, he stopped and examined something embedded in the cliff face. He let go with one hand and tugged at whatever it was, causing Hrodi to gasp.

"Boss! Careful!"

Finally, Nick worked the item loose, put it between his lips, and descended the cliff. On the ground, Hrodi handed him his shirt and shoes.

"What is it? What did you find?"

Nick removed the object from his mouth and held it up in the moonlight. "Well that's interesting." He handed it to Hrodi.

Hrodi looked the item over. It was round and about the size of a silver dollar, but thin and filmy and dull green. It glinted in the moonlight. "A troll scale! But how's that possible? What about their curse?"

"I'm not sure," Nick said as he rebuttoned his shirt. "But what I do know is, the intruder wanted us to think it was a clumsy break-in by Skyrgámur, at least long enough to get away with his real objective."

Hrodi's forehead furrowed. "But if a troll was in the workshop, what would he be after? Unless..." His eyes widened.

"Right," Nick said. "Let's go check on Hulda."

At the rear of the workshop, the roomy stables smelled of newly-hewn spruce and fresh-cut hay. In their stalls, the reindeer munched happily from bags of oats while elves combed their fur or rubbed their hooves clean with towels. Each reindeer gave a snort and a nod to Saint Nick as he passed by. Nick called to each one in turn.

"Ho, Dancer!" he bellowed. "Staying out of trouble, Comet?"

They went down a long hallway with doors lining either side. Finally, far from the bustle and noise of the rest of the workshop, they reached an ornately carved wooden door protected with a huge sliding wooden bar. Two elves standing sentry outside it saluted when Nick and Hrodi approached.

Nick lowered his tone to just above a whisper. "How's she doing?"

"We pushed in her food dish this morning," one of the sentries reported back at the same subdued volume. He pointed at a swinging door at the bottom of the main door. "But she hasn't pushed it back out."

Nick and Hrodi exchanged glances. "And you didn't report that?" Hrodi asked.

The other sentry shrugged. "Maybe she's sleeping late. She does that from time to time."

"When was the last time she sent out an egg?" Nick asked.

The first sentry rubbed his chin in consideration. "Yesterday, about mid-morning. She's late today."

Hrodi frowned. "Should we unbar the door, Boss? Interrupting her will mean she won't lay for at least three days."

"I know it," Nick replied. "But I think we have no choice. We have to see if she's okay."

Nick grabbed the slide bar and pushed it until it cleared the door with a thunk. Hrodi gently pulled the door open. Inside opened onto a large round chamber with a circular pool inlaid in the center, tiled in creamy white. Lamps on tables suffused the space in a soft light, and the walls were decorated with ornate mirrors and Baroque oil paintings with scenes of swans and other birds. Various perches and cushions and seats covered in white velvet were spread around the chamber, and the air was perfumed with a vanilla fragrance. In front of the door, a china plate of mashed peas sat untouched.

Nick stepped over the plate and looked around. "Hulda? Are you in here, girl?" He glanced in the pool and checked behind seats and tables.

From the door, Hrodi called, "Any sign of her, Boss?"

"Not a thing," Nick said.

"Don't forget to check the nestbox," Hrodi suggested.

"Oh, right," Nick mumbled to himself. From under a velvet-covered roost at the rear of the chamber, he slid out a long box lined with dried grass. He put his hand into the grass and fished out an egg, holding it up to the light. It was white-blue and smooth and about the size and heft of a potato, and veined with silver.

Nick exited the chamber and handed the egg to Hrodi. Nick's face burned crimson behind his white beard. "They interrupted my vacation. They invaded our workshop. And they've stolen our elf-swan."

"What are you going to do, Boss?" Hrodi breathed.

"Ready my armor, Hrodi. And hitch up my sledge." He pounded one meaty fist into the open palm of his other hand. "I'm flying to the Troll Kingdom. And I'm going to get Hulda back if I have to pound every fucking troll in the place."

"Armor. Sledge. You got it, Boss."

Nick raised a finger, as if remembering something. "Oh, and Hrodi, one more thing before I go, in case this takes longer than I expect."

"Sure thing, Boss. What do you need?"

"Send some flowers to my wife. Something classy. You know what I mean."

"Got it. One requesting-forgiveness bouquet to Mrs. Claus at the Setai Hotel."

Chapter Three

Nick jumped down from the sledge onto the snowy ground at the edge of the Forbyr Forest, light on his feet despite the full complement of armor he wore. Made by elfcraft, the silvery plate was lighter than it appeared, and fitted together as smoothly as a Saville Row suit. It gleamed in the rising sun, Nick's white beard flowing out from under his great helm, while his long red cape, trimmed with white fur, flapped in the stiff breeze.

After circling the forest a couple times, he'd realized there was no good spot to land in the dense canopy of spruce trees except around the castle in the middle, manned with troll lookouts along its battlements. And coming down right next to the castle and giving up the element of surprise seemed like a bad idea. *A hike through the forest it is, then,* he thought.

He lifted the visor on the helm and unhitched Donner and Blitzen so they could browse the grass tufts poking up here and there through the snow, or nibble on the shrubs running up to the treeline.

"Okay boys, I hope to be back by nightfall, so don't wander too far." *And back in Miami before Anya gets pissed,* he added to himself, a picture of his wife flashing in his mind with her luscious figure, her shining violet eyes and a coy smile, standing before him in whatever mysterious lingerie she'd purchased. The reindeer grunted and bent their heavily antlered heads to graze.

Nick hefted his Ulvehammer and set off into the still dark wood, the rough trunks of the spruce rising ceaselessly before him like the mighty columns of some vast, primeval fortress.

* * *

Inga gazed out the window of her tower as the rising sun sent its feeble beams from far to the south. Made of filigreed ice, her tower rose slender and twinkling above the massive parapets of Troll Castle, a delicate and incongruous contrast to the castle's coarse gray stone and crude, block-like construction. From her chair, she could see across the endless spruce of the Forbyr Forest, a dark green carpet stretching to the horizon. Not that it mattered if one did reach the end of it, for the trolls were cursed from leaving.

She had not slept well, and had risen before dawn. Her son had recently begun setting out on long overnight camping trips into the Forbyr Forest, a development Inga was not entirely comfortable with, although Groschen insisted the boy was old enough and it was perfectly safe. *I won't be truly at ease until I know he's back at the castle safe and sound,* she thought.

There was a place in the forest that she kept her eye on. While it was still dark, she had observed a shooting star, and it had appeared to land in a particular spot in the trees. She hoped the spot wasn't where Roscoe had put up his tent, although she reasoned with herself that it would be unlikely. While she watched the place, she absent-mindedly worked a ball of ice between her fingers, stretching and shaping it.

From the castle below came roars of stupid laughter interspersed with shouts of malevolent glee. With each fresh interruption to her thoughts, Inga's irritation grew. *Good Lord,* she thought. *Are they already getting into the spruce beer? The sun hasn't even been up an hour.* As if to punctuate her point, a peal of inane howls and giggles sounded, echoing up from the castle walls.

Disturbed, she rose and held up her ice creation in the sunlight. A perfect ice tiger sparkled, tail stretched long and ears back as if it were about to pounce. She smiled to see her work. "Tyger, tyger, burning bright," she said, and placed the exquisite sculpture on a shelf next to a furry little ice lamb. The shelf stretched all the way around her apartment, covered with thousands of little animals and people, and even whole scenes of towns or landscapes.

Inga smoothed her amethyst-colored dress, speckled with ice crystals, and descended the long stairwell to the castle. *Maybe Roscoe will already be back from camping,* she thought. At the bottom of the stairs, it was not difficult to follow the idiotic brays to the cavernous throne room of her husband, where several dozen of his troll lieges stood around a large cage, hooting and rattling its iron bars. A few used sticks to poke at something inside. She gave only a brief, disgusted glance at the burly trolls, with their oversized jade bellies squeezing out underneath dirty jerkins, their scaled skin but furry faces, their loathsome yellow catlike eyes. They quieted when they saw their queen, and parted to let her approach the enclosure.

Inside, a beautiful swan with feathers of purest white and a glossy black beak roosted on a rotten log, holding its head atop its long, gracile neck at as dignified an angle as it could manage in the circumstances. It kept its eyes half-closed and peered down its beak in a way that seemed disdainful, as if to open its eyes entirely would be to admit the situation was at all acceptable. *Poor thing, trying to mind its own business and surrounded by idiots*, Inga thought. *The least I can do is rid it of these tormenting fools.*

Inga curled her lip and spoke in her most contemptuous voice. "A swan? That's what's entertaining the lot of you so much? Are you fucking kidding me?" She sent a hard stare around the troll circle. The trolls averted their gazes under her withering glower. "All of you, back to whatever it is you're supposed to be doing."

A few of the trolls shrugged and others began to wander off, muttering under their breaths. "Old Lady Killjoy strikes again." "Just trying to 'ave a bit of fun." "Never met a party she couldn't throw a wet blanket on."

Padded steps walked in from behind her, their pace light and measured compared to the clumsy clomping of the other trolls. "Do you like her, my love?" a sniveling voice echoed through the throne room.

"Groschen." Inga did not bother turning. "Wherever did you find this pitiful waterfowl, and why on earth did you bring it here?"

"Our latest acquisition!" the troll king said brightly. He took a place at the cage next to Inga and rapped the bars with his penguin femur. "This, my dear, is the solution to our problems!"

"I never asked for a pet," Inga said. "I said I wanted to go on vacation."

"Yes, yes, that's right. And this is how we'll do it! You see, this is the elf-swan that the sainted Nicholas uses to power his travel."

Inga regarded her husband. "You've gone fucking loony. Or has word that Santa uses reindeer to pull his sleigh not yet reached Troll Castle?"

"Of course he uses the reindeer," the troll king said. "But how do you think he makes them fly? Not something reindeer are naturally known for you, you have to admit. But this creature"—he indicated the swan with the penguin femur—"produces magical eggs. If I understand the process correctly, all you have to do is grind them up, and ta-da! Elf dust."

"Oh, I see." Inga's eyes widened. "And we can use the elf dust to travel."

"Yes, you're getting it," the troll king said.

Inga shook her head. "But Groschen, we don't have any reindeer."

"No matter," the troll king said. "It's an enchantment. We just have to enchant something suitable to our situation, and it should work the same way." He stroked the scraggly, sickly green beard hanging from his chin. "Although for some reason, we can't get her to lay an egg."

"Probably because you're not giving the poor thing any privacy, you moron. Do you think any woman wants a bunch of boys watching her at her most personal moments?"

"Mom!" came a cry from across the room. Inga whirled and held out her arms as her son came running up.

"Roscoe, you're back!" She lifted him up in a hug. The boy was handsome in his black trousers and a short-sleeved leather jerkin, with his thick mop of blond hair and skin tinted only the palest green cast to reveal his troll heritage. "How was your camping trip?"

"My camping trip?" The troll king jerked his head and gave the boy a meaningful look from over Inga's shoulder. "Oh, right," Roscoe said. "Yeah, I had a good time on my *camping trip.*"

"I hope it wasn't too cold for you overnight," Inga said, setting Roscoe back on his feet.

"Not for me. You know I hardly notice the cold, Mom."

"That's true. I suppose you get that from me." Inga leaned over and peered at a bloody spot on they boy's arm. "Oh no! Roscoe, you've injured yourself!"

Roscoe gave a quick glance to the wound. "Oh, that. I was, er, climbing a tree."

"It looks like you've ripped out a whole scale," Inga said. "Doesn't it hurt?"

Roscoe shrugged. "Not too much."

"Well, we'll put a poultice on it later." Inga extended a hand toward the swan, which she didn't notice had fixed the boy with a decidedly unfriendly stare. "What do you think of the new addition to the castle?"

"Hm, a swan." Roscoe bit his lower lip. "It's alright, I guess. Can I go to my room? I have some things I want to see to."

"Of course," Inga said. Roscoe ran off into the castle, and Inga spun on her heel.

"You know, my dear," the troll king began tentatively, "this would be the perfect time—"

"Don't even think about it," Inga said, swishing away.

The troll king remained alone, stroking his beard. "Privacy, eh?" he finally commented to the swan. "I suppose I can arrange that."

The swan only glared back at him with cold, resentful black   eyes.

Chapter Four

Nick removed his great helm and carried it under one arm, but it hardly helped. Sweat still ran down his temples and rosy red cheeks, and beneath his undershirt he could feel it trickling down his sides. The Forbyr Forest was dark and cool, but he'd been hiking through it for hours wearing a full set of armor and carrying a five-foot warhammer.

From above, he'd estimated it would take about three hours to cross from the edge of the forest to Troll Castle, but he'd been underway at last twice as long. Far from storming the walls and crushing troll skulls with his Ulvehammer in time to grab lunch from their larder, it was already late afternoon with no sign he was any closer than he had been hours ago. He was tired, thirsty, hungry, and irritated, and increasingly suspicious that some enchantment in the forest was turning him around without him realizing it.

"I've gotta be getting closer," he grunted as he stepped over a rotting log. The fallen tree had created a break in the canopy that sunlight shafted through, and tiny winged insects flew up and down the light beams. A gnat buzzed in his ear and he tilted his head to his shoulder to swat it away. Something larger landed on the back of his neck. He reached up with the arm his helm was under to slap at it, but the helm slipped free and rolled down an incline.

"Fuckin' A!" Nick roared. He clasped his hammer in both hands and swung it at the nearest tree trunk. It smashed into the rough spruce bark with a splintering thud that echoed through the trees and bounced back, leaving a deep square indention in the trunk.

He took a deep breath and patted the tree apologetically. "Sorry about that, buddy. Just letting off some steam." He made his way down the hill and bent over to retrieve his helm from where it'd settled in the crotch of a tree. With his ear close to the ground, he thought he detected a burbling sound from somewhere in the distance.

He followed the burble and in a few minutes came across a sluggish little stream that had eroded the ground in its meanderings, exposing the black roots of spruce trees along its way. Nick carefully picked his way down to a flat place along the bank. He set aside his hammer and helm and knelt, cupping his hands to bring the tea-colored water to his lips.

"Well, it's no IPA, but at least it's cool and wet." He slurped down another mouthful and ran a handful of water through his hair. "And I haven't seen this stream before, so maybe I'm making more progress than I thought."

Feeling better, he pushed himself back to his feet and blinked. "Is that what I think it is, or am I hallucinating?" He peered through the tree trunks. Not a hundred yeards away was a clearing filled with lavender and larkspur, and in the middle stood a tidy little cottage with white shutters and a thatched roof.

"What kind of inbred would live way the hell out here, in the middle of the fucking Forbyr Forest?" He retrieved his hammer and helm and jumped across a narrow place in the stream, clambering up the bank on the far side. "To answer my own question, the kind of inbred I'm about to meet."

Nick put his helm on and balanced his Ulvehammer. Alert to any danger, he entered the clearing. And halted at the edge, his jaw dropping in surprise.

* * *

The troll king gripped Hulda's graceful neck in one hand and held her body in the other, carrying the struggling swan down a dark, twisting stairwell. Her little webbed feet bicycled in the air as if she could force her captor back up the stairs.

"So you want privacy, do you?" he sniveled. "Peace and quiet? Have I got the place for you, heh heh. Nobody will ever find you down here, believe you me."

At the bottom, the stairs opened onto a dank, gloomy stone chamber. High overhead, light filtered wanly from a grate, while water dripped down into a stinking puddle in the middle of the floor. The troll king dropped Hulda brusquely.

The swan bent her head up and regarded the troll king. "Awk-awk?" she asked.

"Yes, that's right, this is your new home now. Look, you even have yourself a pond." The troll king pointed to the puddle. "What more could a swan want? Now get to laying."

The troll king turned and started up the stairs. The swan looked to the left and the right and trumpeted a low, mournful awk.

The troll king stopped with his foot on the first step. "What's that supposed to mean? Filthy? I spent all day cleaning this place out. Do you know how many mouldering skeletons I had to haul off and how many spiderwebs I had to sweep away?"

The swan responded with an awk even sadder than the first.

The troll king rolled his eyes and resumed his ascent. "Well, lay a goddamn egg and maybe I'll bring you up for some fresh air," the troll king called back over his shoulder. As he continued trudging up the steps, he grumbled to himself. "Don't know what the damn bird's complaining about anyway. It can lay any time it wants. Look at me, I haven't gotten laid in twelve years and you don't see *me* honking about it."

* * *

Around the cottage's garden, a wrought-iron fence adorned with curlicue patterns bordered the flowers. A sweet wildflower scent perfumed the air. Butterflies fluttered and bees buzzed around the expanse of lavender and larkspur. And in among the plants, a stunningly round and tempting derriere wiggled in the air, covered by a green and orange floral patterned sundress that rode up to reveal well-toned pale green legs. The derriere's owner bent over, working a wood-handled weed remover into the black soil, cutting around the root of a tenacious dandelion. "Come on, get out of there, you damn thing," a sweet voice sing-songed.

Nick removed his helm and cleared his throat.

"Oh!" the voice said, and the gardener stood, revealing a gorgeous older troll woman, streaks of gray only enhancing the allure of the cascades of curly jade hair pouring down her back, the granny glasses at the end of her nose calling attention to her sea green cat-like eyes, her sundress tight enough to flatter the curves of her hips, and its bodice falling low enough to expose the top of a generously-sized green-freckled bosom.

"I'm sorry to startle you, madame," Nick said with a slight bow.

"Oh, not at all," the lady troll said. "It's just that I don't get many visitors out here."

"Do you need any help with that vicious weed?" Nick asked.

"Ha! I think I'm good." The lady troll eyed him up and down and a hint of a smile twitched the corner of her lip. "Believe me, at my age, I know how to strip things down right to the root."

Nick raised an eyebrow. "I've no doubt about that."

"But look at how rude I'm being," the troll lady said. "Chatting away while you're obviously parched and famished. Can I invite you inside for a tall glass of lemonade?"

Nick considered a moment, weighing the threat this woman might pose. *She is a troll*, he thought. *But she seems harmless enough. Surely a drink of lemonade won't hurt.* "I'd be honored, madame."

The lady troll indicated an open gate framed by an arbor draped in honeysuckle vines. "You can come through there. And no need for the formality. Please call me Groa."

Nick passed through the gate and up a little path of irregular paving stones. "Good to meet you, Groa. You can call me Nick."

"I suspected as much," Groa said. "Your fame is spread wide, Saint Nicholas." They reached the handsome door to the cottage, painted a rich saffron yellow and with a round stained glass window depicting green vines on a red background. Groa pointed to his warhammer. "You won't need that inside. You can leave it out here."

Nick's eyes narrowed. "I think I'll take it in with me, if you don't mind."

Groa shrugged. "Whatever you want." She opened the door and ushered Nick in with a welcoming gesture.

Inside, the cottage was one large room, with kitchen, living, and sleeping areas distinguished only by furniture and fixtures. Still, the place was much less rustic than Nick had expected, with modern appliances in the kitchen, electric lamps, and floors of polished dark wood. Neat bundles of herbs hung from the ceiling and shelves overflowed with books and jars of jellies or pickled vegetables. Lacquered pottery with exquisite designs stood on side tables or made attractive exhibits as free-standing items. A soft, gray-haired cat purred around Nick's legs.

"Please, have a seat," Groa said, indicating a plush leather sofa. "Remove some of that armor, if you wish."

Nick set the warhammer and helm on the floor but left his armor on. The sofa proved to be extraordinarily comfortable as he sank into it. Groa handed him a tall glass of lemonade with tinkling ice cubes. Nick gave it a suspicious sniff but detected nothing unusual. A sip revealed it to be crisp and sparkling, and he quickly drained the whole glass.

"How do you get electricity way out here?" Nick asked.

"Solar panels, how else?" Groa answered as she busied herself in the kitchen. She returned in a moment with a plate of tarts, their succulent berries almost glowing on beds of browned sweetbread. Nick popped one covered with blueberries and thought he had never tasted anything more delicious.

"Anything more?" Groa asked. "You finished that lemonade in a hurry. Perhaps you'd like to continue with something...a little stronger?"

"You're too kind," Nick said. "But I really should be going soon."

"Oh, but you just arrived," Groa said. From a sideboard covered with liquor bottles and crystalware, she held out a bottle of Oban 18-year scotch. "Is this to your liking?"

"Ho ho! I suppose one drink wouldn't hurt," Nick said, eyeing the bottle's label. "Where do you get Oban out here?"

"Really, Nick—may I call you Nick?—you make it sound as if I should be living as a primitive. You, of all people, should know you can get anything delivered nowadays." Groa used tongs to pull out ice cubes from a freezer next to the sideboard and dropped them in two crystal tumblers. She poured liberal helpings of the golden liquid over the top of the cubes.

Returning to the sofa, she handed Nick his tumbler and settled on the cushion next to him. She held up her tumbler and the crystal glinted in the lamplight. "Cheers."

"Cheers," Nick said, clinking Groa's tumbler and taking a sip of the smoky, spicy scotch. It went down smooth and cold, but warmed his belly when it landed. "Now that's tasty."

"Indeed." Groa put a hand on Nick's armored knee. "Now, if you don't mind my asking, what brings you to the Forbyr Forest? And so long after Christmas?"

"Heh, not that many trolls are on my nice list even during the yule season," Nick said. "Although there is Roscoe, of course. He's a very good boy."

"Ah, the queen's son," Groa said, moving her hands down his legs. "Let's get those heavy boots off. Your feet must be sore after walking so far."

The boots fell to the floor with twin clunks and Nick had to admit it did feel good to have them off. He stretched his toes luxuriously in the thick wool rug in front of the sofa. "So you're in touch with the trolls at the castle?" he asked.

"I don't see my cousins often," Groa said. "In fact, I don't get many callers out here at all. Especially not ones as charming as you." She had moved back up his legs and somehow managed to unlatch the greaves from his calves, and was working on the tassets covering his thighs. When she leaned over, Nick had a clear view down her dress, and it was obvious she was unrestrained by clothing underneath.

"Yes. Ahem." Nick struggled in vain to avert his eyes from her green-flecked, sumptuously firm breasts. "Well, I'm here looking for something."

"Ah. And what is it you're seeking?" Groa worked now on his breastplate, her hands underneath it deftly locating the straps and connection points.

"I'm searching for...a swan," Nick said, unsure of how much information to reveal. "You know, I'll really need to put all this armor back on in a short while."

"So you've lost a swan," Groa said. "It's noble of you to go looking for such a humble creature."

Nick's eyes fixed on a straw broom in a corner. The shaft was knotted and unsanded, the bristles looped to it by a bright red length of rope. But it was what was on the bristles that caught Nick's attention. They were covered in grayish white rock dust, like the rockspill at the warehouse.

Nick straightened. "Your broom."

"Yes, what about it?" Groa asked. Her fingers danced from the now loosened breast plate up to the pauldrons on his shoulders. "I used it to sweep the dust from my front walk just this morning."

"Oh, the rock pathway. Of course." Nick relaxed. That explained the rock dust perfectly. After a full day with no food, the whiskey was starting to go to his head. Groa's fingers felt good over his doublet. He thought they'd feel even better *under* the doublet.

"You know, it's not long until the sun will go down," Groa said in a low tone. "And you're so tired after your long day. It really makes sense for you to sleep and restart your journey to Troll Castle in the morning when you're fresh." She leaned over and whispered in his ear. "I think you'll find my bed is the most comfortable place around."

"That does make sense," Nick conceded. "Maybe in the morning you can show me the best way to get there?"

"Don't worry, baby. I'll show you the fastest way possible." She had almost finished removing his doublet, and Nick was pushing the straps of the sundress over Groa's shoulders. The dress slipped down her torso easily, and she waggled her hips to shake it the rest of the way off. She slid her way back up Nick's body and wetly kissed his neck along the edge of his beard, while her hands combed through his chest hair. Nick's mouth found Groa's lips, and she eagerly opened them to him.

Still, as they proceeded, something at the back of his mind seemed off to Nick. Something about the connection between the rock dust, and Roscoe, and how Groa knew he was headed to Troll Castle without him telling her. *But then where else would I be going in the Forbyr Forest?* he thought. *Ah, worry about it in the morning, old man, and enjoy the moment.* He ran his fingers lightly down the light green skin of Groa's back and she arched herself into him with a moan, pressing her breasts against his chest. She freed his codpiece and this final piece of armor hit the floor with a clatter.

Chapter Five

Nick awoke grudgingly, for every time he drifted into consciousness, his throbbing head and nauseated stomach sent him back to a dreamland where they didn't hurt. But despite his best efforts, he gradually regained his senses. He noticed first his bone dry mouth, pasted with a cracked coating of scotch and bile. Then the hard, unyielding pillow under his head. After that, something cold and metallic around his ankles, and a nip to the air that was cold even for him.

Not quite ready to risk opening his eyes to see why it was so chilly, he walked his fingers along his body, determining that he wore only boxer shorts. He reached down and scratched around his scrotum. At least there was one satisfied area of his body. Finished with that job, he fished for a blanket to pull up, only to find his arm swinging through free air. It was at that point he decided it might be worth opening an eye to investigate the situation.

"Ugh. Did we finish the whole damn bottle?" he groaned as he screwed open an eyelid.

And quickly closed it again.

And slowly re-opened both eyes. He was in a narrow, dank cell, with raw stone walls and iron bars along one side. On the other side of those bars, a pot-bellied but otherwise gangly, jade-furred troll peered in at him, a tuft of green hair wisping at the top of his head, yellow cat-like eyes watching his every move, a broad, close-mouthed grin plastered stupidly across his furrowed face.

"If you're Groa, you've gotten a hell of a lot uglier since last night," Nick said.

"Good morning, Sunshine," the troll sniveled. "And you hurt my feelings. Surely you haven't forgotten your old friend Groschen? Why, you even attended my wedding!"

"I only came because your bride was my wife's old roommate," Nick said.

"Well, I suppose that explains why the man with a whole workshop of elves only managed to bring a Cuisinart as a wedding gift. But as for Groa, I'm sure she'd like to look in on you." He turned his head and spoke over his shoulder. "Groa, come over and wish our dear Saint Nick a good morning. Don't be shy, now, come on over and let him see you. And bring those clothes with you."

Groa appeared at the bars with a faint, guilty smile and carrying a bundle under one arm. "Good morning, lover?"

"You. Bitch."

She half shrugged her shoulders. "I did what I had to do. Groschen came to me the day before yesterday and told me you might be stopping by."

"You used a love potion on me," Nick growled.

"Not at all," Groa said. "I admit to a disorientation spell to keep you wandering around the forest. But the day I can't seduce a man weakened from hunger and exhaustion with a bottle of scotch is the day I hang up my garters for good."

Nick swung himself to a sitting position on the bench. Chains cuffed to his ankles spilled to the cold stone floor with a clank. The shift in posture almost pushed the contents of his stomach up his throat, but Nick swallowed it down and pointed to the bundle. "Just push my fucking clothes through the bars."

Pieces of underwear and quilted doublet fell to the floor. Nick grabbed his thermal underwear but found he couldn't pull them over his legs because of the chains. He flung them to a corner of the cell in frustration.

"If it means anything to you, that was one wild night of lovemaking." Groa sighed and stared longingly at Nick's crotch. "I mean it, Nick. I haven't had a night like that for simply decades. You rocked this old troll witch's world."

The troll king cleared his throat. "Er, yes, thank you, Groa. That will be quite enough. You can go now."

"You know, if you ever want to stop by again—"

"I said, that's enough!" the troll king commanded.

Groa turned and shuffled away. Nick thudded his rear end back on the bench and gave her a hard, resentful glare as she retreated.

"Don't take it so hard, my dear Saint Nicholas. She really had no choice." From the wall by the cell, the troll king produced Nick's warhammer, holding it up tauntingly. "I've always wondered what it would feel like to hold this fabled item."

"The Ulvehammer!" Nick launched himself at the bars and thrust an arm through, the suddenly taut chains around his ankles nearly tripping him in the process so that his head slammed painfully into the iron shafts.

The troll king danced back a step. "Uh, uh, uh!" He clasped the haft in both hands and tested it with a short, awkward swing. "You know, I always thought this would weigh more."

"Imagine that metal head swinging into your teeth."

"Oh, you're saying that even at this weight it does a lot of damage?" the troll king said. "Or do you mean that swinging it repeatedly in battle makes it feel heavy after awhile?"

"I mean I'm imagining it swinging into your teeth, smashing them into a thousand little pieces like Chiclets," Nick replied.

"Ah, and there's the charming attitude that makes you such an icon to millions of children around the world." The troll king let the Ulvehammer drop to the stone floor, where it landed with a ringing clank, just out of reach of Nick's cell. "Well, ta-ta for now! Don't worry though, I'll be down later for another round of mockery and condescension."

The troll king waltzed merrily away, tapping his long green fingers together while humming "We Wish You a Merry Christmas."

* * *

Inga strolled briskly down the corridor and stopped outside Roscoe's door. She wavered over whether to go in or not. Roscoe had been so distant from her lately, when before they had always been close. All of a sudden, he'd been spending a lot of time on his own in the Forbyr Forest, staying away all day and even spending the night outside. Probably just a phase he was going through, one of those parts of growing up. Inga had made up her mind to keep going and leave the boy in peace when she hesitated again at the sound of a whimper from inside the room.

Is Roscoe crying? She tilted her head and listened. It did sound like somebody was weeping in the room. She knocked lightly and when she heard no answer, opened it and poked her head in.

Roscoe lay on his bed on his side, his arm hooked under his pillow, his face red and his eyes puffy.

"Hey, buddy, everything all right in here?" Inga asked.

"Mom!" Roscoe sat up straight, wiping tears from his face. His eyes narrowed. "Can't you knock before you open the door?"

"I'm sorry," Inga said. "I did knock. You must not have heard it. Can I come in?"

Roscoe shrugged. "I guess."

Inga entered and sat on the edge of the bed. Roscoe's room was clean and well-organized for an eleven-year-old boy. His belongings gave insight into his interests: shelves holding Lego creations in the shape of ice caves, walls lined with posters and pennants with the polar bear mascot of the Toronto Maple Leafs, and his bedside table stacked with books on polar explorers like Roald Amundsen and Sir Ernest Shackleton. Long, cross-country skis and poles stood in a corner, along with sacks for a tent and a sleeping bag.

Inga smiled at her son. "You know, when I was your age, I ran away from home."

Roscoe's eyes widened and he scooted himself over to sit next to her. "You did? Why?"

"Oh, I suppose I was confused. I'd just discovered I could control ice, but I still wasn't very good at it. I thought I'd hurt some people close to me with my powers, and running away just seemed like the best option."

"How long were you gone?" Roscoe asked.

"Three days," Inga answered. "Finally, your grandfather had to come find me. I was miles from the palace. I'd made a little ice fortress for myself, way back in the trees."

"Weren't you hungry after three days?" Roscoe said.

Inga laughed. "I suppose I was."

"And Granddad made you go back to the palace?"

"He didn't *make* me," Inga said. "We had a talk. He explained that everybody understood any harm I'd caused hadn't been on purpose, and anyway, I hadn't seriously hurt anyone. That everybody missed me, and if I came back with him, we'd all work together to figure my powers out."

Roscoe nodded. "Mom? Can I tell you something?"

"Of course," Inga said. "You can tell me anything."

Roscoe bit his lip, deciding whether to go on. Finally, he plunged in. "Mom, I'm the one who stole the swan."

"What?" Inga said. "What do you mean? Where did you find it?"

"It was at a workshop, like where elves work. I was supposed to sneak in and take her, but something went wrong and I accidentally broke a window. And I had this gross spoon I left behind, to provide a false trail, Dad said."

"So 'Dad said,' did he?" Inga forced her voice to remain calm. "But how did you get to the workshop? How did you know where to go?"

"I went to Auntie Groa's, and she gave me a broom of hers that flies," Roscoe said. "And I sat on it, and the broom seemed to know where to go."

"Roscoe." Inga put her hand on her son's. "You know it's wrong to take something that doesn't belong to you?"

"I do know it, Mom. I didn't want to steal the swan. But Dad said it had to be me, because I was the only one troll who isn't affected by the curse, on account of my human blood. And he said I shouldn't tell you, that you'd just be worried if you knew, so it should be a secret."

"I see," Inga said, seething inwardly.

"Am I in trouble, Mom?" Roscoe asked.

"No, honey, you're not in trouble." Inga put an arm around Roscoe's shoulder and hugged him to her. "I'm sorry your father asked you to do that."

"You won't talk to him about it, will you? Then he'll know I told you."

Inga sighed. "Oh, honey, I'm sorry. I have to talk to him about this. But I won't say you told me. I'll say I figured it out."

Roscoe pursed his lips. "You know what, though? I do feel a lot better now that it's not a secret anymore."

"I'm glad to hear that." Inga pushed herself off his bed. "And no more camping trips for a while, okay, Roscoe?"

"Okay, Mom." When her hand was on the door handle, he spoke again. "Mom? Was this talk kind of like the one you had with Granddad?"

"Yeah, it was, kind of," Inga said. She entered the corridor and shut Roscoe's door behind. She gritted her teeth and balled her fists. *And now for a talk with Groschen that's going to go a whole hell of a lot differently.*

* * *

Nick's head felt a bit better, his pounding headache down to a mild pulsation. A troll guard had brought a tin cup of yellowed water so he had rinsed the acrid taste from his mouth as well. He'd slipped on his doublet and laid back down on the hard bench for an hour or two. For a while he stared up at the dull gray stone that surrounded him. *Thursday morning,* he thought. *One day to get out of this fucking troll prison and back to Miami where I belong.*

Nick imagined arriving back at the hotel to find Anya just getting back from the beach, the curve of her bikinied ass perfect as she bent over to retrieve a box from the dresser. Anya putting her finger to her lips and smiling, slipping into the bathroom to change, with a promise to be out in just a minute. And after an excruciatingly long wait, the knob of the bathroom door turning and the door slowly opening....

Nick's reverie was interrupted by the sound of a heaving sob that seemed to come from the next cell over. He waited a moment listening, and when no further sounds came, closed his eyes again. "Let's see," he mumbled. "The bathroom door was opening, and—"

The honk of a blowing nose intruded, followed by quiet sobs. Nick sighed and gingerly sat upright, testing his queasy stomach. When that went well, he rose and shuffled to a small barred window in the wall, his leg restraints clanking with each step. It was hard to see with no more than a lone flickering torch from somewhere outside for illumination, but he could just make out a child-sized figure hunched in the corner of the neighboring cell.

"Hey," Nick said softly. "Hey, is everything all right in there?"

The figure looked up, tears flowing freely from wide eyes over a huge, veiny nose and into a scraggly white beard. "Th-they took me spoon. They took me spoon and they wouldn't give it back!"

"Why, you're Skyrgámur, aren't you?" Nick said. "The yogurt-gobbler."

"That's right," the bearded figure said. "And what good's a yogurt-gobbler without his spoon? His very, very, very special spoon."

"Are you sure you didn't lose it?" Nick asked. "Maybe at a workshop somewhere?"

"No! I would never lose it." Skyrgámur jumped up and stamped his foot. "First, I was minding me own business in the kitchen in this dumb old castle. I like to visit castles like this late at night, so's I don't disturb nobody."

"Yes, I know," Nick said.

"So, I was just taking a look-see around the kitchen to check if they had anything tasty in the works. Well, most of what I finds is some nasty old meat and some rotten cheese. Don't they have nothing sweet? I says to myself. And that's when I found it."

"Found what?" Nick said.

"A huge kettle of the tastiest, creamiest yogurt I ever come across. Full of chunks of raspberry, all tangy and ripe and bursting with flavor. And raspberry being me own special favorite, you know. Well, I dug in and started scooping it up as fast as I could, letting that cold, creamy concoction coat me cuspids." Skyrgámur's story trailed off as he remembered the delicious yogurt, his eyes staring off into space.

Nick cleared his throat. "So what happened then?"

"Well, I haven't gotten more'n two or three spoonfuls in me mouth when I feels something grabbing me arms and pulling me away. I struggled and struggled, but it's two of them big brute trolls they have here, and gripping me arms like iron. And they takes me to the throne room, where that skinny old troll was sitting in a big chair, rapping out a rhythm with that bone of his."

"That'll be the troll king, I expect," Nick said.

"Exactly so," Skyrgámur said. "And he rubs his green bean fingers together and gives me some speech about how he's trapped me with his superior intellect and I fell right into his trap and whatnot, and then they... then they..."

"What did they do then, Skyrgámur?" Nick asked gently.

"They took me spoon!" Skyrgámur wailed. "And they tossed me in here, where I been ever since." The pitiful gnome dropped to the floor, tears flowing.

"Shh, calm down," Nick soothed. "I know where your spoon is."

Skyrgámur looked up with reddened eyes. "You do?"

"Yes, I do. And I can give it back to you, but only if we can get out of this prison."

"Well, how are we going to do that?" Skyrgámur asked.

"That's the part I'm working on," Nick said. "We just need a lucky break."

Chapter Six

Inga stomped down the corridor of the castle until she reached the door to the troll king's sleeping chamber. She wrenched the door handle and threw it open, letting the heavy oaken timber slam against the stone wall. "Groschen!" she barked, but no one answered. She muttered to herself, "Damn it, you're not in the kitchen, you're not in the armory, you're not in the throne room. How am I supposed to bawl out your scrawny green ass?"

A beam of midday sun edged around the curtains and shone on the bed, where a long lump hid under the covers. "Ah, ha! I see you hiding in there, you cowardly bastard. How dare you use our son to do your dirty work?"

When the lump didn't respond she tramped over and yanked the blankets back. Underneath was a sack, roughly her size, straw stuffing poking out in places, and wearing a blue dress with ice crystals on it.

"Wha? This is one of my dresses." Inga lifted the sack. White strands of yarn stuck out from the top of the sack, tied in a long braid, and two sewn-on blue buttons made for eyes. A crude mouth drawn on with lipstick in the shape of an O completed the face. "Oh my God, is this supposed to be me?"

Inga dropped the sack. From the nightstand she picked up a magazine with a photo of a platinum blonde woman wearing a Santa hat in a snowy landscape. The woman was otherwise unclothed, and covered her naked breasts with her hands while she gave a disdainful, sneering look to the reader. Inga read aloud the title and cover copy. "'Ice Queens Unleashed. Your chilliest fantasies inside. Pulse-pounding sex action with a sensual selection of snowy, slutty sweeties. Blizzard blowjobs and snowjobs.' Gross! How is this even a real publication?"

She dropped the magazine and picked up a wadded white cloth from the nightstand, holding it in the light beam. "What's this?" She let it unfold into its natural shape. "A sock?" Her jaw dropped in realization. "Ooh, and it's all crusty!" She flung the sock away with a shudder of revulsion and fled the room.

"Eaagh! Nasty! Disgusting! Groschen, when I get my hands on you, I'm going to throttle that bony little neck of yours!" she yelled. Under her breath, she added, "Right after I wash my hands in scalding hot water for about half an hour."

* * *

Roscoe crept down the stone stairwell, clutching a little bag of dried corn kernels. As he descended, he whisper-called, "Hulda? Are you there? Don't be mad at me. I brought you a treat."

At the bottom, he glanced around the labyrinthine cellblock, lit only by an occasional flickering torch, water dripping from various spots in the ceiling into stagnant puddles. Slimes and fungi spread across the stone surfaces, and the iron bars of the cells rusted in their grooves. This was the deepest, oldest part of Troll Castle. Roscoe tiptoed along the rows of cells. Most were empty, except for the occasional reclining skeleton or scurrying rat.

Finally, he came around a corner and heard a sniffling from one of the cells. Roscoe perked up and hurried over to it. "Oh, there you are. I brought you a treat."

But when he reached the cell, he jumped back in surprise at the little, white-bearded gnome waiting for him. "Me spoon? Did you bring me spoon?"

"Uh, no," Roscoe said. "You're not who I expected to be here."

"So it's time for me lunchtime gruel, then," the gnome said.

"No, I didn't bring that, either." Roscoe studied the gnome, who wore a little yellow coat with a double row of buttons, red breeches, and a tight-fitting red cap. "I have some corn kernels here, if you want."

"Bah." The gnome waved a hand and turned around, hopping up on the cell's sleeping bench.

"What did you do to be imprisoned down here?" Roscoe asked, but the gnome only stared at him resentfully. Roscoe shrugged and continued on his way, stopping to inspect a huge hammer that for some reason stood in the middle of the corridor.

A voice cleared its throat and Roscoe spun around, only to jump back again at seeing a rotund, white-bearded figure standing at the bars in the next cell.

"Hello, Roscoe." The man looked down at him with a gentle smile. He wore only red boxers with reindeer on them and a quilted doublet.

The boy blinked several times. "Santa Claus?"

"The one and only." Santa chuckled. When he looked at Roscoe, his eyes held both kindness and fire, as if he could see right into the boy's heart. "Have you been a good boy lately, Roscoe?"

"I...I..." Roscoe quickly changed the subject. "Wh-what are you doing here?"

"Waiting for my lunch, of course," Santa replied.

As if in response, a husky troll with rolls of belly fat squishing out from under a filthy leather jerkin and leather breeches at least a size too small came lumbering around the corner. He held a pail in one hand and two dirty clay bowls in the other.

"Hrrn. Master Roscoe. Didn't expect to see you down here," the troll rumbled.

Roscoe put his hands on his hips. "Stunker, why is Santa Claus being held prisoner?"

"Don't know. Caught invading castle, I expect. Should ask your father." The troll dropped the pail to the ground with a dull clunk. He bent over and ladled cold, gray gruel into one of the bowls, ripping a vicious moist fart in the process. He shoved the bowl under a gap in the bars at the bottom of the gnome's cell.

"Hmph," the little gnome grumbled. "Have to eat it with me fingers, I suppose."

Stunker ladled the second bowl full and slid it into Santa's cell.

"Could I get a spoon for this?" Santa asked.

"Nope." Stunker pushed himself back to a standing position with a groan and emitted a wall-rattling belch. "Best come up with me, young master," he said to Roscoe. "Not sure king wants you down here."

"Why can't the prisoners even have spoons to eat with?" Roscoe asked.

"Yeah, why can't I have me spoon?" the gnome echoed.

"King told me no silverware," Stunker said.

"Well, what if I went up to the kitchen and brought down two spoons for them?" Roscoe asked. "Dad didn't tell *me* not to give them silverware."

Stunker scratched his head with a thick green finger. "Guess it'd be okay." He shrugged, hefted the pail, and lumbered off.

"Great," Roscoe said. "Hold on, you two. I'll be back in just a minute with spoons for you."

"Use somebody else's spoon? That's really more me brother Thvorusleikir's department," Skyrgámur said, but Roscoe had already dashed away in the opposite direction from Stunker.

* * *

"Where the fuck is he?" Inga's stomping had grown half-hearted as she passed down yet another corridor of the endless dank, ill-lit corridors of Troll Castle. "And for that matter, where's everybody else? Usually I can't walk two goddamn steps in this place without some clumsy troll oaf almost bowling me over."

She crossed an empty storage chamber filled with dusty and cobwebbed furniture and stopped to lean against a pillar and catch her breath. "I've been walking from one end of this giant hovel to the other for hours," she exhaled.

As she leaned, she heard a distant roar and enthusiastic hoots. Immediately Inga perked up and cocked her head. "Aha! Found you assholes." She pointed down a corridor and resumed her stomping.

She emerged into a large, round chamber lit by barred windows and a hanging candelabra. Tapestries covered the wall, depicting troll heroes of the past committing various acts of violence, cruelty, and sheer stupidity.

"The east assembly hall? But I've already searched here. And now the noise has stopped." Inga slowly spun in the center of the room, listening. Her eye alit on a tapestry of Overivrig the Gigantic, the famous troll who went into a battle rage so fierce he beheaded the whole enemy host with his great sword, not to mention the entirety of his comrades and allies. The tapestry showed a troll with a rather stupid surprised expression holding a bloody sword amid a forest of headless figures, still standing, blood spraying from their necks. Inga rolled her eyes.

From behind a small, triangular wooden door built into a stairwell came a high-pitched cackle. "Groa?" Inga said. "In the broom closet?" She crossed the room and pressed down the iron latch. Slowly the door swung outward. She had to duck to enter.

Inside the cramped space, Groschen and Groa stood on either side of a circular portal opened in the back wall of the closet, its edges a glowing rainbow swirl. The last members of a procession of trolls armed with axes, maces, and clubs were just stepping through the round opening, Groschen directing them through with his penguin femur like a conductor with his baton. Groa held a broom over the outer rim of the portal, sparks flowing between the bristles and the buzzing magical disk.

"What's this?" Inga asked. "Where are they all going?"

"Ah, hello, my dear. A little excursion, that's all." Groschen continued to circle his femur.

Inga's mouth hung open. In her surprise, she'd forgotten all about her anger over Roscoe. "But...how?"

"No, my love, you mean How*burg*," Groschen said.

Inga peered through the opening. Indeed, behind the trolls rose a snow-covered hill with a tidy community of pink Victorian houses rising along its slopes, all turrets and balconies and gables. The houses jumbled around a cozy, central square, where children in mittens and scarves skated on a little ice rink. Around the rink's edge, residents and tourists in fuzzy earmuffs bought steaming mugs from sidewalk vendors or strolled along arm in arm, little suspecting the calamity that was about to occur.

"You see," Groschen explained, "this morning our new swan was good enough to lay one of her magical eggs. So with the resulting elf dust and the help of my lovely cousin—" Groa gave Inga a wave with her free hand—"I decided to take the opportunity to exact my long-awaited revenge on the contemptible citizens of our hated enemy."

"Hated enemy?" Inga said. "Howburg?"

"Yes, of course, who else?" Groschen said. "The ones who so unjustly laid the curse on me and my kin that's kept us confined to our own land for far too long."

"But, that was decades ago," Inga said. "Most of the people there now probably don't even remember what happened. Most of the people there now probably weren't even *alive* when it happened."

"It matters not." Groschen flipped his femur in the air and caught it again. "They've benefited from the curse all along just as well as if they'd fully taken part."

"Benefitted?" Inga blinked. "By you not invading them?"

The last troll passed through and Groschen followed, waving his femur up and down and humming a marching tune.

"Groschen, wait!" Inga called. Her face reddened and her eyes narrowed. "You promised me a vacation. But you're using the elf dust on this, instead!"

Groschen took a glance back, one leg through the portal. "Er, yes. We'll get to that vacation someday, my dear. First things first!" He resumed his humming and trooped on, flipping on a pair of heart-shaped sunglasses as he passed into the bright snowy landscape.

"You never intended to take me on a vacation at all, you bastard!" Inga shouted after him, but Groschen paid her no attention.

"Ooh, tough luck, sweetie." Groa stepped around and walked through the portal. As soon as her broom lost contact with the edge, the portal began to shrink. "Ta-ta, Inga," Groa sang back. The portal rapidly shrank to the size of a soap bubble, then disappeared with a pop.

"Groschen...you...you green-hued, bad-breathed, crayon-dicked, lying fucking asshole!" Inga screamed helplessly at the spot in space where the portal had been. She kicked an empty bucket in the corner, sending it flying into the wall with a clatter. "How can you think of revenge before you think of your wife?"

"Mom! Mom!" came Roscoe's voice from outside.

Inga ducked her head through the triangular door and looked out in the assembly hall. "Roscoe? What is it?"

"Mom! I was down in the dungeon and—"

"Roscoe! You know you're not supposed to go down there!"

"Sorry, Mom." Roscoe sighed and almost vibrated from the excitement of the story he was holding inside. "I was looking for the elf-swan."

"And you found it in the dungeon?"

"No, not her," Roscoe said. "But when I was down there looking, I found Santa Claus in one of the cells! Dad is keeping him prisoner down there! And also, this one other weird leprechaun kind of guy."

"Nick, er, Santa's here?" Inga said.

"Yes, and they want me to bring them spoons." Roscoe held up two large metal spoons. "Also, why are you in the broom closet?"

"Just looking for your father." Inga stepped out. "Well, let's go down and have a look."

Chapter Seven

"They used the elf dust to get to Howburg?" Nick said to Inga and Roscoe, who stood outside his cell. "That's bad news. If little Cindy Sue's curse is broken, the trolls will tear that place apart in no time. The town will be lucky if there are any survivors."

"Plus, Groschen was *supposed* to use the elf dust to take me to Vail," Inga said.

"So can you help them, Santa?" Roscoe asked.

"I'd like to." Nick kicked a foot, rattling the chain against the floor. "But as you can see, I'm not going anywhere."

From the cell next door, Skyrgámur's spoon clinked repeatedly as it struck against the clay bowl while he hungrily shoveled the gruel into his mouth. "Not as good as yogurt, but at least it fills me tummy."

Down the corridor, Stunker appeared at an intersection, trudging along with his now-empty pail.

"Stunker can help!" Roscoe said. "Hey, Stunker!"

"Huh?" The troll turned to see where the voice came from. "Master Roscoe, you're still down here. And Missus Inga, too." He made a clumsy bow to Inga, releasing a long, growling fart as he bent at the waist.

"Stunker, come on over." Roscoe waved the troll over to them.

"Oh, don't invite the smelly brute any closer," Inga muttered.

"It's okay, Mom. He may be smelly, but he's really nice."

In any case, Stunker was already trodding heavily in their direction, his exposed belly fat jiggling under his leather jerkin with each step. "What you need, young Master?"

"Do you know where Dad keeps the keys for the cells?" Roscoe asked.

"Always keeps keys close, on person," Stunker said. "In back pants pocket."

"Well, do you know if he has an extra set anywhere?" Inga prodded.

"No, no extras." Stunker scratched his head and gave Roscoe and Inga a suspicious look. "Why you ask so much about keys?"

"Let me ask you a question, Stunker," Nick said from behind his cell bars. "Why aren't you with the rest of the trolls invading Howburg?"

Stunker's face fell. "Other trolls never let me take part in fun. Say I don't smell good enough. 'Mop this, sweep that,' they say. 'Carry gruel to dungeon. Wash clothes. No, don't come with. Have floors scrubbed by time we get back.'" A thin, poignant fart slipped out from his rear. "As if they smell much better."

"That's a good point," Inga said. "None of you are exactly a bouquet of violets."

"If I find a way to get out of here, will you help us stop the invasion?" Nick asked Stunker.

Stunker bobbed his head. "Yes, I help. Why should other trolls get fun all the time while poor Stunker do all work? But without keys, how you leave cell?"

"That's a good question," Nick said. "Maybe you have a crowbar somewhere, and we can try to pry open the bars?"

At that moment, Skyrgámur appeared next to Stunker. "Well, while you all figure that out, I'll be up in the kitchen taking a look around for that kettle of yogurt what's so tasty."

"Skyrgámur," Nick said with forced patience. "How did you get out of your cell?"

"Why, I used me new spoon!" Skyrgámur held up the metal spoon, the handle of which had been bent and twisted into a pointed instrument.

"Do you think you could you do the same thing for my cell?" Nick asked.

"Well, I'm in a bit of a hurry, you see," Skyrgámur said, already spinning around to start off down the corridor. Before he could take a step, Stunker slipped a thick finger in the waistband of the gnome's breeches, and Skyrgámur pumped his legs only to find he wasn't going anywhere. He glanced back to check what the problem was.

"Santa. Cell. Open." Stunker said. He lowered his head and gave Skyrgámur a hard stare.

"Er, right." Skyrgámur stepped to Nick's cell and stuck the pointed end of the spoon into the key slot, fishing around inside. "I suppose I can fetch me snack later."

* * *

Groschen hummed as he led his troll army up the snowy path to the little town of Howburg. He waved his penguin femur around like a baton or threw it spinning up in the air, catching it again with perfect timing.

Groa cackled at his side as they marched, twirling her broom around gleefully. "What fun!" she chortled. "After so many scores of years gardening at that shack in the woods, now to have so much excitement!" She sighed deeply. "Still, it's a shame we couldn't work something out with the big, strapping fellow."

"My dear cousin," Groschen said. "If you're referring to that overblubbered toy-shucking oaf Saint Nicholas, it'd be best if you put him out of your head altogether. I've outwitted him once and for all, and he's quite securely locked away, never to spread Christmas cheer again. He'll rot in my dungeon until the memory of him is completely faded from the earth. I'm a bit surprised at you, to tell the truth."

Groa looked as if she'd been slapped in the face, but then she straightened. "You know what? When you're right, you're right, cousin," she said. "Imagine an old witch like me, mooning over an oversized elf like a teenager who just had her cherry popped. Why, now that I think about it, I must appear contemptible to you."

"I wouldn't go that far," Groschen said. "A bit sentimental, that's all. Ah, here we are."

The troll army had reached the ice skating rink, and all activity came to a stop. Skaters halted in mid-skate, little children clasped their parents' hands, tourists held their coffee mugs halfway to their lips without taking a sip, even friendly roaming dogs sat back on their haunches. All paused and turned to stare at the motley force that had entered their town. The trolls stood in a line two-deep, menacing with their nasty-looking weapons, their huge bellies, their shabby furs and ill-fitting leather jerkins, all wearing cheap plastic sunglasses in the bright sun.

"Citizens of Howburg!" the troll king cried, raising his penguin femur theatrically, though the dramatic effect was somewhat undercut by his heart-shaped sunglasses. "The day that you've long dreaded has arrived. You've enjoyed decades of fraudulent peace, but now the time for your righteous come-uppance is here. You may meet your fates bravely, or make it fun for us and rush around in a panic. In either case, prepare for your utter destruction!"

A little boy being held by his mother popped his thumb out of his mouth. "Mama, what that green bean man talking about?"

"I'm sure I don't have any idea," the boy's mother replied.

The citizens laughed and returned to their various activities, apparently deciding the trolls in the sunglasses were some sort of prank or club.

"Alright, boys," Groschen snivelled, pointing to the town. "Let 'er rip."

* * *

"I don't know." Skyrgámur sat at Nick's feet, poking the tip of his spoon into the keyslots in the shackles around Nick's ankles. The cell door hung open and Roscoe, Inga, and Stunker leaned back against the bars while the gnome worked. "The cell door's one thing. And I could unlock the chains from the ring in the ground. But these around your legs have wee little openings, so's I can't get me spoon into them at all."

"Ow!" Nick winced. "You jabbed me again."

"Sorry about that. I just don't know if I can do it. I need me proper tools for this job."

"You know what?" Nick said. "Let's skip this. The door's open, and I'm unlocked from the ground. I'll just have to keep the fetters on until we find the troll king."

Nick stepped out of the cell with the chains dragging behind him. He grasped the Ulvehammer and gave the floor a solid tap. The ringing resounded through the dungeon. "Lord, it feels good to have this back in my hands. Now which one of you can lead us out of the castle?"

"I'll do it!" Roscoe jumped up and the others followed. With Roscoe at the head, they made their way out of the labyrinthine dungeon and up a long, dank staircase, Nick's chains jangling along the floor all the while. At the top of the stairs, they proceeded down an endless corridor of gray stone and through innumerable dim halls and chambers. Decoration was sparse and tended toward dark-colored tapestries and murals depicting scenes of bloody, exaggerated violence.

"Do we have time for a wee visit to the kitchen?" Skyrgámur inquired.

"No!" the others replied in unison.

"How big is this castle, anyway?" Skyrgámur asked. "And have the trolls ever thought of investing in some lamps to brighten this place up?"

"Bright light hurt troll eyes," Stunker explained.

"Don't worry, we're almost to the front gate," Roscoe said. "Just four more corridors."

"This is why I really prefer staying in my ice tower," Inga said. "At least up there I can get some sunlight."

"I hope we get there soon." Nick checked his Blancpain watch. "Mid- afternoon already. And today's Thursday. Anya's going to kill me if I don't get back by tomorrow."

"What are you so worried about?" Inga asked. "Aren't we taking your sleigh? We'll get to Howburg in no time."

"It's not that easy," Nick said. "I left my bag of elf dust at Groa's cottage, along with my armor. The reindeer should still have enough magic left to fly here, but we wouldn't be able to fly away. We'll have to hike through the Forbyr Forest to retrieve my stuff."

"Groa's cabin lies hours from here," Inga said. "We might not get there until late tonight."

"Maybe we should fortify ourselves for the trip with some yogurt?" Skyrgámur suggested.

"Are you really going to hike through the woods at night wearing only those boxers and a doublet?" Roscoe asked Nick.

"I'll be all right, Anyway, what can you do?" Nick's face lit up with a thought and he guffawed. "Ho ho! At least I have the chains to keep my ankles warm."

Hulda sat on a crate in her dim underground chamber, sadly regarding the water dripping from the grate overhead. She missed her cushions and her mirrors, her paintings and her perfect little tiled pond, all perfectly designed for a very special swan like her. *This* place, on the other hand, was a dump. She wondered if she would ever see her old room again.

From somewhere in the distance came a metallic clank. She cocked her head. Yes, there it was again, continuous now, as if pieces of iron were being dragged along the ground. And there were voices along with it.

It wasn't exactly the same sound, but something about the ringing reminded her of sleigh bells. A vision of the white-bearded man in his sleigh with the reindeer appeared in her head. A kind man, who always had a treat and a gentle word for her.

"Ho ho!" came a rumbling laugh through the grate.

It really *was* him, the white-bearded man, come to rescue her and take her away from this awful place! Hulda began shouting, "Down here! Down here! Down here!"

"Awk! Awk! Awk!" came the trumpeting honk through the corridor.

Nick halted and looked around. "Hulda?"

"The swan!" Roscoe's voice quavered. Nick's ears pricked, sensitive to the slightest sign that a child might be feeling guilty.

"Do you know where she is?" Nick asked. Roscoe didn't speak. Nick put his hands on Roscoe's shoulders and looked him in the eye. "Roscoe, if you know anything about how we can get to her, you have to tell me now."

"I'm... I'm not sure where Dad put her," Roscoe said.

Inga was already trying the heavy wooden doors along the corridor, but each was locked. "This stupid castle! Why does Groschen insist on keeping everything locked all the time, anyway?"

"Keep talking, Hulda!" Nick shouted. "We're on our way!"

"Awk! Awk! Awk!"

"Can you pick the locks?" Nick asked Skyrgámur.

"All of them?" Skyrgámur said. "I could, but it would take me all day. Can you narrow it down?"

"Over here!" Stunker pointed to an iron grate in the floor. "Sound come from here."

Nick was there in an instant, moving faster than anybody would have expected from such a big man. The sound of awk-ing was indeed much louder and clearer over the grate. This was a low spot in the corridor, where moisture from the stone walls and floor collected and trickled down.

"Awk! Awk! Awk!"

"We're almost there!" Nick called. He fell to his hands and knees and inspected the grate's iron rods. "This is going to be heavy as shit," he muttered. He looked up at Stunker. "Can you help me lift it?"

Stunker nodded. "I help."

"Good troll," Nick said, already back on his feet and giving Stunker a clap on the back. "Okay, you take that side and I'll take this one. Remember to bend at the knees so you don't pull a back muscle."

He and Stunker squatted and gripped the bars. "On the count of three," Nick said. "One. Two. Three!"

They hefted the grate, their hamstrings flexing like melons on the backs of their legs, the sinews in their forearms taut and corded as steel cables, their neck bands straining like rope. They groaned with the effort, Nick's face flushing red and sweat beading down his temples, while Stunker's face turned a deep green. Slowly, with a deep scrape of metal on stone, the grate lifted. When they had brought it knee high, Nick grunted out, "Toss it to the left!"

They heaved it to the left, where it landed with a thunk that shook the floor. Nick rose and wiped his forehead and Stunker emitted a long, burbling fart.

"You two did it!" Roscoe cheered. A trumpeting "awk!" came from below.

Nick exhaled. "Now we just have to figure out how to get down there and retrieve Hulda."

"Maybe I could find some rope?" Inga suggested.

"Just leave it to me," Skyrgámur said. In a blink, he had dropped himself over the edge of the shaft and shimmied his way down the sides. A moment later there was a splash and a surprised "awk!" followed by a scrambling sound. Skyrgámur's head poked above the opening and he climbed out, an elf-swan nearly his own size tucked in one arm. Skyrgámur grinned. "Stealing things is me specialty."

"Hulda!" Nick cried, and the swan leapt from Skyrgámur and flapped to Nick, landing in the crook of his arm and giving an affectionate peck on his cheek. "Hi, girl, I'm glad to see you too. Let's get you home as quick as we can."

"But we still have to walk all the way to Auntie Groa's cottage," Roscoe said.

"That's true," Nick said. "Unless Hulda is ready to lay an egg."

The elf-swan shook her head sadly.

"Skyrgámur, what's that in your pocket?" Inga asked, narrowing her eyes at the gnome, who had folded his arms high across his chest, as if hiding something.

"Me pocket? Why nothing, I'm sure," Skyrgámur said, slowly backing up.

"No, I believe there's a lump in there." Inga dove and grabbed Skyrgámur before he could leap away and slipped her hand inside his yellow coat.

"Hey!" Skyrgámur protested. "Leave me private areas alone!"

Inga ignored him and pulled her hand back out, holding up a silver-veined egg triumphantly. "Nothing in there, eh?"

"No fair!" Skyrgámur said. "Finder's keepers. I found that lying unattended and it belongs to me."

"And *I* found it in your pocket, so now it belongs to *me*," Inga said. "But I'm giving it to the one who can make use of it." She handed off the egg to Nick's waiting hand.

"Ho ho!" Nick said. "Looks like we won't need to walk after all."

Chapter Eight

Groschen flipped his penguin femur in the air and whistled as he strolled through Howburg, watching with approval at the unfolding destruction. Everywhere his gaze fell, glass was shattering, cars were burning, people were running or screaming and otherwise panicking as the trolls leveled their town. Sirens blared and dogs barked hysterically.

"Keep up the good work, Sneglehode," he called to a troll in dirty furs breaking up the ice rink with a huge axe, each blow spiderwebbing the frozen surface. Little children holding their ice skates sobbed around the rink's rim.

"Way to go, Ormertå," he urged a long, knotty troll who had climbed up to the second story of a cute Victorian house holding a flaming torch. Ormertå held the torch to the curtains blowing through a broken window, while in the tidy yard his compatriots held back the stricken elderly owners of the house by their arms.

"Have fun, Skittensinn!" he encouraged a lean, grinning, shirtless troll who carried a shrieking young woman over his shoulder, her long hair flying as she beat on his muscled back. "You might try that clump of bushes over by the church."

Groschen eventually stopped in the middle of the town square and slowly spun, sighing contentedly as he took in the devastation taking place all around him. "Marvelous, just marvelous."

"Hey, Groschen, there you are," came Groa's voice from the direction of the town cemetery. "You're going to love this. Look who I found hiding behind a tombstone."

Groschen turned to see and his jaw dropped. Groa tugged along a little girl by one hand through the cemetery gate. The girl had a blonde bob cut topped with a pair of red ribbons. She wore pink pajamas with lacy fringes at the sleeves and ankles and pink fuzzy slippers. But her most noticeable feature was her long-lashed big blue eyes, opened wide and bloodshot from crying. A smile curled the corners of the troll king's mouth.

"Why, if it's not little Cindy Sue!" Groschen said.

"That's not my name," the little girl said. "Cindy Sue's my great-grandmother. My name's Riley."

"Riley. Of course it is." Groschen squatted so he'd be at eye level with the girl. "You're your great-grandmother's spitting image, did you know that?"

Riley nodded.

"And where is your great-grandmother now, Riley?"

"I'm not telling you." Riley jutted her chin. "You're a bad man."

"I'm actually a bad troll," Groschen said. "A very, very bad troll. Do you see everything that's happening here?" He gestured at the chaos around them. "These are all my friends, and they're doing this because I ordered them to."

"Well, you should order all these trolls to stop what they're doing and go back where they came from." Riley glared at the troll king defiantly.

"I'll tell you what." Groschen put a hand on the girl's shoulder. "You tell me where your great-grandmother is, and I'll tell all the trolls to stop. Do we have a deal?"

Riley shook her head.

"Do you want me to make her talk?" Groa cackled. "I have some special tricks I've been saving for just such an occasion."

"I don't think that will be necessary." Groschen pushed himself off his knees up to his full height. He held out his hand. "Come with me, Riley." When she didn't move, Groa shoved her forward, and Groschen grabbed her little hand with his long green fingers.

"No! I don't want to go with you!"

"Too bad, you're coming anyway." Groschen yanked her along the sidewalk on the outside edge of the cemetery fence. Behind the cemetery where the town edged up to a little wood, a shiny white water tower rose into the sky. Across the round water tank at the top, the town's slogan spread in cheery red script: *Welcome to Howburg. Just How You Like It.*

Groschen parked Riley in front of the ladder attached to one of the water tower's outer support pillars. "Climb," he demanded, pointing up to the water tank one hundred and fifty feet above them.

"I don't want to," Riley said. "It's too high."

"I said *climb*," Groschen growled. "Or I'll hand you over to the witch." Groa gave the little girl an evil smirk and slowly waved her hand one finger at a time, emphasizing the long crimson fingernails contrasting against her green skin.

"Eep!" Riley eeped, and started climbing.

"Good choice," Groschen said, following her up the ladder.

***

Nick's sledge came to a smooth landing next to where his companions waited on the rampart at Troll Castle. He stepped off wearing his full armor, gleaming silver in the light of the setting sun. His long cape, of a deep scarlet velvet with white fur trim, flowed behind him in the brisk wind, as did his long white beard from under his silver great helm. In one hand he gripped the Ulvehammer, in the other a small leather pouch. Below the mighty castle walls the trees of Forbyr Forest stretched endlessly into the distance.

Donner and Blitzen snorted and tossed their antlered heads where they stood harnessed to the sledge, proud to see their master's magnificent appearance. Hulda gave an approving "awk," Roscoe and Stunker cheered, and Inga let out a long, low whistle. Only Skyrgámur failed to look up from the big pot of yogurt he was shoveling into his mouth.

"Anya always was the lucky one," Inga breathed. "To think, she got to marry the hunk, while Father insisted I marry that string bean troll."

"Everybody ready?" Nick checked his blue-dialed Blancpain watch. Even with the elf dust, it'd been a time-consuming process to call the reindeer, fly bareback to where he'd left the sledge and hitch them up, and retrieve his armor from Groa's cottage. Now night was already falling, the eve of Anya's birthday. This whole venture was taking a lot longer than he'd anticipated. "Climb on and find a spot."

Nick took the reins and sat on the middle of the bench. Inga and Roscoe squeezed in on one side of him, and on the other, Skyrgámur took a place with his yogurt pot. Stunker waggled his ample rear end between Skyrgámur and Nick and plonked down. The force of Stunker's seating popped Roscoe right off the bench at the other end.

"Hey, there's no room for me!" Roscoe said.

"Sorry," Stunker said. "I make room." He lifted one cheek and expelled a long poof of gas with a descending pitch like a trombone. A noxious cloud enveloped the sledge.

"Oh. My. God." Inga said, pinching her nose.

"Hey, you're curdling me yogurt!" Skyrgámur complained.

"What do you know? I do fit now," Roscoe said, wedging himself in.

Nick was about to lift the reins when an irate "awk" came from the side of the sledge.

"Oh, sorry, girl," Nick said. "Why don't you ride on Roscoe's lap? That would save some room."

"Oh, could she really?" Roscoe said.

Hulda poked her swan head over the floor of the sledge and gave Nick an annoyed look.

Nick shrugged. "You could always ride on Stunker's lap if you prefer. But pick now, because this train's about to leave the station."

Hulda gave a disdainful glance at Stunker and flapped up to Roscoe, who wrapped an arm around her with a smile on his face.

"If we're all settled, let's get going," Nick said. He glanced from the leather pouch to Stunker and back. "Hmm, taking into account the weight load, maybe a double dose."

With a flick of his wrist, elf dust scattered from the pouch and sparkled all around them as it settled, a pleasant gingerbread aroma replacing the lingering stench from Stunker's emission. Nick snapped the reins. "On Donner, on Blitzen! Dash away, dash away, dash away all!"

The reindeer scrambled and the sledge lurched and slid down the rampart, faster and faster, the landscape becoming a blur as they took off into the air with an exhilarating feeling in their stomachs that made Inga and Stunker gasp and Roscoe yelp out in glee.

* * *

Riley shivered and clutched her arms around herself. The night was chill, and though her pink pajamas were made of heavy flannel, they still could not keep the wind atop the water tower from whipping right through the fabric. Riley considered asking the troll king or troll witch if they could provide her with a hat or coat, but decided against it. She wasn't going to ask *them* for anything.

Groschen patted the railing along the water tower catwalk. "Come, Riley. Take a look."

Riley didn't move.

"I said, come take a look," Groschen said vehemently. Groa tapped her fingers against the side of the water tank, her nails clicking against the metal. Riley hurried beside the troll king.

"It's a beautiful night, isn't it?" Groschen gestured at the stars, clear and bright in the black sky.

"Mmm," Riley shivered.

"And down there, such a gorgeous tableau." Groschen indicated the town spread out before them, where columns of smoke rose from numerous raging fires, red and blue lights flashed from overturned police vehicles, and people ran in panic with armed trolls chasing after them. From this height, the screams, sirens, and frantically barking dogs sounded distant and faint. "I've dreamed of this for more years than you can imagine, Riley."

"That's because you're a bad man," Riley said. "Normal people think about nice things, not things like this."

"And yet, I can't deny my true nature, can I?" Groschen replied. "Tell me, what did you get for Christmas this year, Riley?"

Riley's eyes momentarily lit up. "Christmas this year was great. I got a new mermaid doll that changes color in the water and who comes with her own comb, and a little stroller with over-sized wheels to push all my dolls in, and a stuffed Persian kitty that really meows, and a new pair of tennis shoes with jewels in them, and a jump rope with pink handles, and a—"

Groschen held up a hand. "Okay, I get it, kid. You know what I got for Christmas this year?"

"No, what?" Riley said.

"I got a big, fat stocking full of zilch," Groschen said. "And that's all I've ever gotten. Nada. Nichts. Nothing. Nothing for Christmas. Nothing for Easter. Nothing for All Hallows Eve. And do you know why I get nothing, Riley?"

"Because you're bad?"

"No, because I'm a troll. And trolls don't get anything we don't take for ourselves."

Riley was silent for a minute. Finally, she said, "I think it's really sad."

"Because I don't get anything?" Groschen said. "I appreciate you saying that."

"No, not because you don't get anything," Riley said. "It's sad because you don't understand. All those holidays aren't really about *getting* things. We only give presents so we can show each other we love each other and make each other happy."

"Well, this year I'm making myself happy by giving myself this present," Groschen said. "The present of destroying your town."

"Look!" Riley pointed into the sky. "A shooting star! And it's coming right for Howburg!"

It was true. The shooting star arced across the firmament, growing larger and brighter as it neared. It dropped lower and lower and finally they lost sight of it when it passed behind the silhouette of a church steeple.

Groschen snapped his fingers. "Groa, could you look into that?"

"It would be my pleasure, cousin." Groa straddled her broom and stepped off the edge of the catwalk. For a sickening moment, the troll witch dropped out of sight, and then floated up again, mounted on the broom. She zoomed off in the direction of the church, her cackle echoing in the night.

Chapter Nine

The sledge glided into the parking lot behind the white, high-steepled church in a shower of snow and elf dust sparkles. Roscoe handed the elf-swan off to his mom and jumped from the bench onto the pavement. "Wow! That was the best trip ever! How fast do you think we were going?"

With Hulda in one arm, Inga stepped gingerly down after him, her face queasy. "Faster than I ever want to go again."

"Ho ho!" Santa roared. "You can't deliver presents to children all over the world in one night driving a garbage scow!"

At the rear of the church, three trolls were spraypainting the walls. *Trolls rule, Howburg drools* read the rounded bubble letters defacing the elegant white-painted wood siding. At the sound of Nick's laugh, they turned and lowered their heads, regarding Nick and his crew over the tops of their cheap plastic sunglasses.

"Hey, it's Santy Claus," one of the trolls said.

"And he's got Old Lady Killjoy and her brat with him," another troll said.

"And Stunker, too," the third troll said. "Hey, Stunker! You got my laundry done yet? You better not have forgotten the fabric softener like you did last time."

"Don't take the bait, Stunker," Skyrgámur advised. "Just ignore them."

"Don't worry, they no bother me," Stunker said,

backing himself down off the sledge.

"Oh, you're about to get bothered." The troll who appeared to be the leader laughed. He was a tall, dark green brute with a red mohawk and wearing a leather jacket. He picked up a bicycle chain from the ground and began swinging it over his head, advancing menacingly toward Stunker. Behind him, the second troll, in a wifebeater undershirt, snapped open a switchblade, while the third, wearing a tracksuit, brandished a crowbar.

"Hey, Stunker," the leader said. "I think you've gone Benedict Arnold on us. You know what trolls do to turncoats, don't you?"

"No, but it sounds like a fascinating subject," Nick said cheerily, interposing himself between the three trolls and Stunker. He rattled the chains around his legs and thumped the head of the Ulvehammer against the ground. "Why don't you boys put down your weapons and we'll have a little talk about where your king is?"

"Well, well, well, if it ain't the fat man himself," the red-mohawked troll said. "I've got a better idea. Why don't you eat shit and die?"

The mohawked troll charged at Nick, bringing the bicycle chain down with a snap. Nick, moving with a speed that belied his bulk, sidestepped him, while at the same time reaching back with his free hand to give a shove that sent the troll sprawling across the pavement. The troll landed facefirst in front of Donner, who snorted and reared his head.

The troll pushed himself up to his feet and picked grains of gravel out from his bloodied cheek. "You're going to regret that, man. I'm going to make you pay!"

Meanwhile, Stunker cracked off a heavy dead limb from

an oak tree at the edge of the parking lot and lumbered over to Nick's side. "Two against three. Seem fair."

From the sledge, Skyrgámur sniffed the air. "I smell something delicious!" He popped off the sledge bench and darted across the grassy churchyard in the direction of the Howburg downtown.

"Skyrgámur!" Roscoe said. "Come back! You can't go by yourself!" He dashed after the gnome.

"Stop, both of you!" Inga yelled as she clambered off the sledge, but to no avail. She ran after them, but there was a rush of wind and Groa swept from the air, landing on her broom right in front of Inga.

The troll witch dismounted and smirked. "Going somewhere, Inga?"

Inga fixed Groa with a hard stare. "Unless you're here to show me where Groschen is, you'd best get of my way."

"Oh, I don't think so, honey," Groa said. "My job is to keep you and that luscious hunk of manhood over there—" she gave a nod in Nick's direction—"from disrupting the trolls' important work here tonight."

"Whatever." Inga stomped across the grass, but Groa lowered her broom like a railroad crossing arm. When Inga reached out to push it out of the way, sparks flew from where her hands met the broom handle and she swiftly withdrew them.

"Nuh uh uh!" Groa sing-songed.

"Don't make me take you out, *honey*," Inga said.

"You and what army?" Groa said.

From behind Inga came a sudden flapping and a fierce "awk! awk! awk!" that startled both women. Hulda landed at Inga's side and emitted a sour honk at the troll witch.

"Me and one pissed off elf-swan, that's who," Inga

answered through gritted teeth.

* * *

"Wait! Wait for me!" Roscoe called after Skyrgámur, who sprinted through the chaotic streets of Howburg with tongue lolling out and brandishing his spoon.

"Can't stop!" Skyrgámur yelled back. "Following the smell!"

The nimble gnome leapt over a pile of bricks knocked from a bank's wall, skittered around glittering puddles of broken glass in the streets, and hopscotched through a mob of trolls fighting against citizens armed with baseball bats. Roscoe managed to keep a few steps behind Skyrgámur but couldn't quite catch him.

Skyrgámur finally stopped in front of a Victorian house painted white and mint green, with comfy rocking chairs on its wrap-around porch. An incredible aroma of baking bread and yeast wafted out the open front door. Its tall, valance-topped windows exhibited elaborate cakes and sugar-dusted pastries. A sign over the door read *La Dolce Pita, Howburg's Finest Italian Bakery.*

"This is it," Skyrgámur breathed. "This is the source." Reverently, he climbed the steps and went through the front door, Roscoe at his side.

The interior was warm and cozy, seemingly spared the tumult afflicting the town outside. Tiffany lamps and chandeliers bathed the space in cheery light, and display cases showcased a grand selection of cream-filled cannolis, jam-stuffed bombolonis, and honey-soaked stuffoli. Behind the front counter, a proprietor in a chef's hat and apron had his back turned to them, using a wood-handled peel to slide something into the open brick oven.

"Excuse me, sir," Skyrgámur said, all but drooling. "Do you think you could provide me with a selection of your scrumptious confections? I've already got me spoon ready."

The proprietor turned around and Skyrgámur and Roscoe screamed. It was a lanky, snaggle-toothed troll, his green face bewhiskered like a cat's and streaked with dried reddish-brown residue, although whether it was blood or jelly wasn't clear. In the back corner of the bakery, a mustachioed man in an apron groaned from where he was slumped against the wall, a hand to a bloody welt on the side of his head.

"Ah, customers," the troll hissed from behind the counter. "What can I poison you with, I mean serve you with, today?"

Skyrgámur backed away. "You know what? I've changed me mind."

"Muggen, what are you doing here?" Roscoe, over his initial shock, put his hands on his hips. "You need to leave this bakery right now and go wait at the town square until we can round all of you trolls up and send you back to Troll Castle."

"Ha, Master Roscoe, you always did have quite the sense of humor," Muggen said. "I've been doing some baking. Would you and your friend care to sample my wares?"

"Well, maybe we could give it a try," Skyrgámur said, cautiously edging forward again.

"Excellent!" Muggen said. The troll pulled something out of the oven with the peel and slid it onto a plate. Beaming, he bent over the counter and offered the plate to

Skyrgámur. The plate was covered with a black, vaguely cake-like mound, worms crawling in and out of the oozing frosting and beetles creeping around its edges. "What do you think of my invention? I call it vermitorta!"

Skyrgámur blanched. "You know, I'm feeling something I've never felt before. I think I'm off me appetite."

"You don't like my creation?" Muggen hissed, his yellow, cat-like eyes widening. "Come on. One little taste couldn't hurt."

"Actually, I think it could," Skyrgámur said.

Muggen had come around the counter with the plate in one hand and a carving knife in the other. He approached Skyrgámur and Roscoe, who backed toward the door. "Research shows you have to try a new food seven times before you can know if you really don't like it," Muggen said.

"Yeah, that's not happening," Skyrgámur replied. "I'm not putting that pile of creepy-crawlies anywhere near me mouth."

"You come in my bakery and dare to insult me?" Muggen hissed. "I'll pluck your eyeballs out and use them in my minestrone!"

"M-my bakery..." came a slurred voice from the corner.

"Shut up, you." Muggen sidled over and gave the man a kick to his gut that produced a gasp of pain.

Roscoe and Skyrgámur had reached the threshold. They gave each other a look and spun, squeezing themselves through the door and shooting off across the porch, down the steps and into the street. Muggen loped after them with the carving knife, his other hand to his head to keep his chef's hat from falling off, hissing and yowling like a cat in a fight. He tossed aside the vermitorta, which thudded against the bakery's mailbox at the street, its slimy, wriggly, black contents dripping down the wooden pole.

* * *

Nick faced the red-mohawked troll with the bicycle chain and his flunky with the switchblade in the snow-patched church parking lot. He shuffled from foot to foot, keeping the Ulvehammer light in his hands and at the ready, while the two trolls circled him warily. When the trolls had positioned themselves on opposite sides, Mohawk shouted, "Now!" and they both lunged in.

Nick ducked, avoiding the swinging bicycle chain, and used his left hand to jab up with the Ulvehammer, catching Mohawk square in the sternum with the face of the fifteen-pound head, producing a sickening crack of bone. Simultaneously, he thrust back with the elbow of his right arm, knocking Switchblade's knife hand aside.

Before Switchblade could strike again, Nick pivoted, bringing the Ulvehammer arcing around. Its antlered spike hooked into Switchblade's shoulder, smashing through the acromion bone at the top of the shoulder blade. Nick jerked the Ulvehammer back, yanking out a mass of tissue. The knife clattered harmlessly to the pavement from the troll's limp hand.

"Which of you wants some more?" Nick asked.

Mohawk took in a ragged, painful breath and coughed, foamy dark blood spurting from his mouth. Switchblade clutched his good hand to his shattered shoulder, where the stringy, dangling ends of muscle fibers and tendons dripped redly down the front of his wifebeater.

Sensing the fight had gone out of these two, Nick took a moment to catch his breath and see how Stunker fared against the troll with the crowbar.

"Not too shabby," Nick said to himself, observing that Stunker had seized his opponent in a bearhug. The other troll, too constricted in his movements to raise his arms, ineffectually whacked the crowbar against Stunker's blubbery backfat, where it bounced off harmlessly. Stunker locked his hands together and squeezed in the small of the troll's back until the spine gave a loud pop and the crowbar dropped to the pavement with a clang.

Stunker released the troll, who flopped to the ground. "I get to laundry later. You take nap now."

A cackling scream and a high-pitched *awk* caused Nick and Stunker to whirl around. Inga had pinned Groa's arms behind her back while Hulda sat on Inga's shoulder, pecking viciously at Groa's face and neck. With each thrust, she took out a chunk of flesh, and blood splashed bright red on the pure white feathers of her long neck.

"Tell me where Groschen is or, I swear to God, I'll let this swan go for your eyes!"

"Okay, okay!" Groa pleaded, twisting her head this way and that in a vain attempt to avoid Hulda's beak. "Call the bird off and I'll tell you!"

"Hulda, that's enough!" Inga commanded. "For now."

Groa exhaled, and her eyes roved to where her broom had fallen. Nick placed his boot over it. "Well, Witch? Answer Inga's question."

"Fine," Groa said. "You'll find my cousin at the—"

A boy's scream pierced the night air. "Roscoe!" Inga cried, instantly letting go of Groa's arms. Groa fell to her knees. "Don't worry! I'm coming, baby!" Inga hurried off toward the town, Hulda still on her shoulder. The swan looked back at the others with a bemused expression.

Nick bent and picked up the broom with his free hand. "Well, I guess we follow her," he said. To the reindeer, he called, "We'll be back in a little while, boys."

Donner and Blitzen snorted and stamped in response.

"I don't suppose it would interest you to know I'm in dire need of medical attention," Groa said, rising and gingerly putting her fingers to the various bloody gouges on her face.

"Do you think there's a medical professional in town who'd be interested in treating you?" Nick snapped her broomstick in half over his knee and tossed the pieces aside. "Start walking."

On their way out of the parking lot, Mohawk staggered toward them, half-heartedly lifting the bicycle chain. Without even stopping, Stunker extended a meaty fist straight in Mohawk's cheek. Mohawk stumbled back and spat a stream of blood, teeth tinkling to the ground. Then he swooned and dropped.

"You take nap, too," Stunker said. "No need to brush teeth first."

They passed Switchblade, who stared at them as he clutched his shoulder.

"You need nap?" Stunker asked.

Switchblade simply shook his head and stepped back to let them pass.

Chapter Ten

Muggen focused on the boy and the gnome trying to escape from him. The small prey had excited his cat-like instincts, and Muggen had tucked the carving knife into a sheath on his belt to allow him to take to all fours, bounding after his quarry. *The brat and his friend are nimble, but I'm the fastest troll at Troll Castle.*

Roscoe and Skyrgámur dodged wildly through crowds of people and obstacles, but Muggen managed to keep just a few steps behind. Hardly anybody stopped to stare and nobody bothered to intervene, as they were all distracted in their own efforts to survive. Bonfires of library books, overturned emergency vehicles, and hysterically screaming women all lay in their paths, but the two kept running. Skyrgámur jumped right on top of a burning Amazon delivery van, bypassing a group of trolls ripping open the packages and quarreling over the contents. Roscoe ducked under two trolls who argued as they tugged at the leg of a pair of designer jeans that was far too small for either of them. Roscoe and Skyrgámur met again on the far side of the van and dashed into an alleyway.

"Out of the way, fools!" Muggen hissed at the trolls with the jeans, bumping into one who tumbled backward but didn't let go, rending the jeans in half with a ripping sound.

Muggen arrived just in time to see Roscoe and Skyrgámur sidestep a pile of garbage cans and bags and launch off a crate to scramble over the wooden fence at the back of the alley. Muggen crashed straight through the garbage as he continued the chase, metal cans rolling away noisily. At the fence he yowled and simply took a huge, cat-like leap over the top.

As he landed on the other side, Muggen hesitated. He had emerged at the town square, with its open, overlapping terraces built around an oval ice-skating rink. Food carts were on their sides or infested with trolls gorging themselves on the contents, while the pretty winterberry holly and yellow-leafed witch-hazel shrubs had been ripped from their beds and scattered about. But where were the gnome and the boy?

Ah, I see, Muggen thought to himself. Blocked from going around the rink by the tipped food carts, they had wandered onto the only area free of chaos: the ice itself, where they cautiously stepped across the slippery surface, holding hands to support each other. *They've made a mistake. They can't possibly escape now.* Muggen rose to two feet and began edging around the rink.

A woman's frantic voice from the far side of the rink attracted his attention. "Roscoe! I'm here! Just keep going!"

Muggen narrowed his eyes. It was Inga, the ice queen, with the annoying magical swan at her side. *Do I dare interfere?* Muggen wondered. But it seemed the ice queen and the troll king were on the outs. The king had rejected her at the portal, all the trolls had seen it. *I think the queen does not enjoy the royal protection anymore. Neither she nor the boy.* He smiled and withdrew the carving knife. *After taking care of the bitch and her brat, I believe I'll take the bird back to the bakery. Roasted swan would be delicious.*

* * *

Groschen paced back and forth on the catwalk, stopping occasionally to gaze out over the town while he rapped his penguin femur against the metal railing in an irregular rhythm.

"You seem nervous," Riley said. "Maybe your plan isn't working out like you expected?"

Groschen shot her an irritated glance. "Well, aren't you awfully nervy for such a little girl?"

"I think you're wondering why your witch isn't back yet. Surely it shouldn't take so long to see where a shooting star landed."

Groschen only grunted in response.

"Great-grandmother Cindy Sue told me about you," Riley said. "She told me if you ever came back, to remember one thing. She told me that no matter how big and important you act, you're really just a coward. So long as we fight back, we're sure to win, because in your black little heart, you're afraid."

"That'll be quite enough out of you!" Groschen thwacked his penguin femur against the railing so hard it split, half of the bone spinning off into the air and landing several seconds later with a pooshing sound in the soft snow far below. Groschen held up the remaining half with a pained expression.

"Aw, your little bone broke!" Riley said. "How are you going to boss your trolls around now?"

"Aargh!" Groschen stomped along the catwalk to the far side of the water tank, out of sight.

Riley smiled and wrapped her arms around herself, hopping from one leg to the other to stay warm. She stared at a burning house in a neighborhood and imagined standing near it, letting the flames warm her body. *Great-Grandmother, if you can hear me, I can sure use your help now. Even if you yourself can't come to help, maybe you could send somebody who can.*

Some shouting from the town square cut through the general din. She peered down and saw two boys skidding unsteadily across the skating rink, one dressed oddly in a yellow coat and red breeches. A cat-looking troll wearing a chef's hat and with a knife in one hand leapt onto the ice after them, only to slide unexpectedly. On the other side of the rink, a blonde-haired woman at the rink's edge called to them. Just then, a white-bearded man in a long red cape arrived at the scene.

"Santa!" Riley whispered. "Thanks, Great-Grandmother, for listening to me."

* * *

Nick, walking with Stunker and Groa, heard Inga yell again for Roscoe at the town square. It sounded like Roscoe might be in trouble. "Make sure Groa doesn't get away," he told Stunker before hurrying ahead.

At the ice rink, he took in the situation. Inga was at its edge, holding out a hand helplessly, as if to pull in her son. On the ice, a long, feline troll in a chef's hat and armed with a long carving knife circled around Roscoe and Skyrgámur, preventing them from moving. The two stood, shaking and clutching each other to keep from falling on the slippery surface, continually turning to keep the menacing troll in front of them.

Nick narrowed his eyes. "Muggen. I should have known."

Nearby, two burly men sat on a bench with forlorn expressions and wearing jerseys that read "Howburg Hockey Club" across the back, their ice skates on the bench beside them. Nick tapped one on the shoulder. "Excuse me, sir, do you mind if I borrow those?" He pointed at the ice skates. "I think they might be about my size."

The man looked up and his face at first took a confused expression, then brightened. "For you, St. Nick? Of course!" He held out the skates.

Nick slipped off his cape and boots, took one of the skates, and bent to slide his foot into it. It fit perfectly.

"Here, let me save you some time," the other man said, squatting in front of Nick to start tying the laces. "Are you here to save our town?"

"I'm working on it," Nick replied, slipping on the other skate and tucking the ends of the ankle chains into the tops.

"What are you going to do on the ice?" the first man asked.

"I see a troll who needs to spend some time in the penalty box," Nick said. The skates tied, he waddled toward the ice. At the edge of the rink, he hefted the Ulvehammer in both hands and stepped onto the ice.

He began stroking and built up speed to a fast glide. The troll had his back to him and was about to pounce on Roscoe and Skyrgámur. Nick barreled into him, sending the cat flailing and yowling across the rink until he thudded into the boards.

Nick looped smoothly around Roscoe and Skyrgámur and skated to a stop, shifting the Ulvehammer to one hand. "Here, take hold." Roscoe took Nick's proffered hand and Skyrgámur took Roscoe's, and together they carefully made their way to where Inga was waiting for them.

Just when they had almost reached her, the hiss of skates came from behind them. Muggen swished in front of them and spun, having switched his knife for a hockey stick. He grinned, and a tooth was missing from his upper gum.

"Does your coach know you're out here?" Nick asked him.

"Very funny, fat man," Muggen replied. He whistled and the hiss of skates came from either side. Two more trolls slid beside him, huge hairy jade bellies spilling out from under Philadelphia Flyers jerseys that were at least two sizes too small. "Meet my enforcers."

"Dumb and Dumber?" Nick said. "Larry and Curly?"

"Grusom and Grådig," Muggen replied. "C'mon, boys. Time for a kill." The three began gliding around Nick, Roscoe, and Skyrgámur.

With a gentle stroke of his ankles, Nick glided up to Grusom. "Hey, ugly, this one's for you," he said, bumping Grusom with his shoulder before skating off. Grusom, knocked off course, corrected himself and took the bait, charging after Nick, Grådig following just behind him.

"No, you fools!" Muggen cried. "We're after the small ones!" But it was too late. Grusom and Grådig were off. Muggen brandished his stick at Roscoe and Skyrgámur. "Don't even think of trying to run." He skated after the others.

Grusom and Grådig caught up to Nick and Grusom body checked him. Nick flew into the boards and bounced off, dazed. The two burly men in the Howburg Hockey Club jerseys, joined by a group of kids in similar jerseys, stood on the other side and booed the trolls.

"C'mon, Santa," one of the kids urged. "Get back out there!"

Nick shrugged the hit off and glided after the enforcers. Hearing the skates coming after him, Grådig spun just in time for the Ulvehammer to strike him in the stomach, bounding off harmlessly.

"Aw, that's a muffin," Grådig said. "That the best you got?"

From behind, Grusom whacked Nick at the base of the spine with his stick, right in the gap between two plates of armor, and Nick arched his back painfully. Grådig hooked the back of his knee, and Nick collapsed to the ice, landing on his side with a thud that knocked the air out of him.

Muggen had caught up with them and circled Nick. "Well, well, well," he purred. "Looks like St. Nicholas is down for the count. Or is that a different sport? I can never keep them straight." He kicked Nick in the gut with the heavy tip of his skating shoe and Nick emitted a groan.

* * *

As soon as Santa had drawn Muggen away, Roscoe tugged at Skyrgámur's hand and they started toward his mom, calling to them from an opening in the boards. But Roscoe also heard another voice, higher-pitched, coming from somewhere in the distance. "Help! Up here!" He looked in the direction the voice came from. *There*, he thought. *It's coming from the top of that water tower.* He squinted his eyes. *It looks like a girl, about my age or a little younger.*

At the edge of the rink, his mom helped pull them up to solid ground. "Oh, Roscoe, I'm so glad you're safe." She enveloped him in a big hug.

Roscoe bore her affection for several seconds before shrugging her off. "Okay, Mom, that's enough."

"What about me?" Skyrgámur asked, arms spread.

"Um, I'm glad you're safe too, Skyrgámur," Roscoe's mom said. Hulda craned her neck over and gave him a gentle peck on the cheek.

"Mom, we've got to go help that girl!" Roscoe pointed at the catwalk at the top of the water tower, where the girl was waving a hand at them. From behind the water tower, a lanky troll appeared, strolling over to the girl and appearing to shush her. "And Dad's up there with her!"

"Is he." Inga's jaw clenched. "Yes, I think we will go pay a visit."

"Tell the girl to get in line." Skyrgámur pointed onto the ice, where the three trolls were repeatedly kicking Santa's quivering body. "The old man needs our help now!"

"But what can we do?" Roscoe asked.

"I help him." Stunker's voice came from behind them. "Just as soon as get feet in these skates."

* * *

Nick closed his eyes and grunted with the impact of each kick by Muggen and the troll enforcers. They'd knocked the plates of his armor askew, exposing the skin underneath. Blow after blow struck him in his hip, his kidney, his solar plexus, his spine. Blood flowed from his nose and a slash across his head. All he could do was clutch the Ulvehammer and hope the trolls lost interest at some point. *Can't hold out much longer,* he thought. *At least Roscoe and Skyrgámur made it to Inga. She'll get them out of here and keep them safe.*

There was a pair of loud thunks and the blows stopped, followed by a hiss of skates that stopped in front of Nick's face. Hesitantly, Nick let one swollen eye blink open and squinted up. Stunker rose above him.

"Come on, Santa." Stunker held out a hand. In his other he held the limb he'd earlier broken off from the oak tree. Grusom was doubled in half nearby, spitting teeth onto the ice. "I be wingman."

"What happened to Groa?" Nick croaked as he took Stunker's hand and stiffly got to his feet.

"Oh, she get away," Stunker said. "We catch later."

Back on his skates, Nick wiped the blood from his eyes, straightened his armor, and scanned the rink. Stunker's attack had frightened off Muggen and Grådig, but they were already regrouping on the far side of the ice. Grusom would recover soon, as well. There wasn't any time to waste. "Follow my lead," Nick said to Stunker.

Nick stroked toward the nearest net, building up speed, with Stunker right behind him. They came around the net and sprinted toward Muggen and Grådig, Nick lowering himself into a crouch. As they approached, Muggen swung his stick at Nick's head. Nick dodged, at the same time reaching to hook Muggen's feet with the spiked end of the Ulvehammer. Muggen danced out of the way and their weapons passed harmlessly by each other. But the flat of Muggen's swinging stick spanked Grådig right in his overhanging gut with a clap that sounded across the rink.

Grådig yelped and held a hand to the bloody, rectangular welt that had appeared on his belly.

"Now that's a slap shot!" one of the burly men shouted from the boards.

Nick and Stunker skated away, only to find that Grusom had recovered and waited for them, hockey stick held over his head like a club. He smirked, and the broken outline of his teeth stood out against the red that burbled from the corners of his lips. Grusom brought the stick down, and Stunker barely had time to lift his tree limb to block it. The heavy oak limb cracked, leaving Stunker with half a stick in each hand.

Nick skated in and out of the traffic and around the net. He came back and crouched for another charge. Muggen and Grådig had the same idea, skating toward Nick with strokes of their feet. For a moment, Nick's gaze met Muggen's from across the rink, and their eyes narrowed. The challenge was on. Nick had the Ulvehammer and the trolls had their sticks at the ready, accelerating toward each other like runaway freight trains. Time seemed to slow and the background blurred as the inevitable collision approached.

"Oy, me spoon!" came Skyrgámur's voice from somewhere in the blur, and a gyrating spoon spun into view, landing on the ice right in front of Grådig. There was no time for him to avoid it, and he skated right over the utensil, sending him head over heels into a flying somersault. Simultaneously, Nick and Muggen crashed into each other, Nick's far greater bulk bouncing the lanky troll in the opposite direction.

Grådig sailed, feet flailing over body, and the blade of his skate met Muggen's throat just as Muggen recoiled at high speed. The blade sliced clean through Muggen's scrawny neck and his head arced, rotating through the air, chef's hat still atop it, blood fountaining from the severed arteries.

"Ohh!" the spectators yelled, cringing in unison.

Grådig's body landed with bone-crunching force, the momentum carrying his limp frame all the way to the boards.

Muggen's head landed with a wet thump on the jagged end of one of the oak limb halves Stunker held outspread in his hands. Stunker and Grusom both stared in shock at the grisly trophy, its yellow cat eyes wide in surprise, its lips pursed in a little O, blood spattered across the white of the chef's hat. The rink was silent for several long moments, and then Stunker and Grusom started laughing, roaring with huge troll guffaws, Stunker doubling over and ripping a huge joyful fart.

The spectators clapped and cheered. "Now that's what I call a hat trick!" came the burly man's shout from the boards.

"Funny, right?" Stunker said.

"Hilarious," Grusom replied. "And you're not a bad troll yourself. I've never really gotten to know you, Stunker."

"You come help us rescue girl?" Stunker pointed to Riley, still waving and shouting for help at the top of the water tower. "But you have to turn against king."

"Sure, why not?" Grusom put an arm around Stunker's shoulder. "I never liked that skinny-ass bastard anyway."

Chapter Eleven

"There's Santa Claus." Riley pointed to the tiny figure of Santa in silver armor and scarlet cape, approaching the town cemetery with his comrades behind him. "He's coming to rescue me and capture you."

"He's doing no such thing," Groschen sniveled. "I anticipated his arrival and made allowances for it in my plans, which you would have known already if you'd considered my unparalleled intellect. His demise is inevitable, I assure you."

"If you say so," Riley said.

"I do say so. But if you simply tell me where your great-grandmother Cindy Sue is hiding we can bypass all this unpleasantness and you can go back to wherever it is you came from."

Riley wrapped her arms tighter around herself as the wind picked up and turned her back to the troll king.

"Have it your way way, then." Groschen descended the ladder from the catwalk. About halfway down, he pulled out a large jar of vaseline from a pocket and began spreading it with his green bean fingers over the rungs, holding on to the side of the ladder with his other hand.

"What is that you're putting on the ladder?" Riley called down through the metal grill of the catwalk.

"Just a little something to give our friends a slippery reception."

"Why do you keep a big jar of it in your pocket?" Riley asked.

"Never you mind that," Groschen snapped back up.

Groa appeared without warning, hovering several feet away from Groschen on her broomstick. "It's because he's a chronic masturbator, dearie," she cackled up to Riley.

"Oh, there you are," Groschen said. "Where the hell have you been?"

"First, I had to tangle with that goddamn elf-swan—not to to mention your bride—who practically destroyed my beautiful features with her ferocious pecking. Just look at what she's done to my face!" Groa swept a hand over her visage, riddled with scabbed wounds.

Groschen gave a disinterested glance. "It'll heal."

"I recommend glazing her with orange sauce and roasting her for three hours in an oven when this is all over," Groa said.

"That seems a little extreme for my wife," Groschen said.

"I'm talking about the swan, you idiot!"

"Oh, right," Groschen said. "That doesn't sound like it should have taken too long, though."

"Well, after that I had a little problem with my broomstick I had to fix." Groa indicated a place in the middle of the broomstick where it was held together with duct tape. "Anyhoo, I'm back now."

"Just in time," Groschen said. "If you'll look in the cemetery, you'll see that the big red oaf, my practically incandescent wife, and their freakish friends are nearly here. Why don't you see if you can do something useful and get rid of them?"

***

Nick strode on a stone path through the tombstones, his cape snapping in the chill evening wind, the chains dragging in his wake. Inga stamped a few paces behind him, her glare never leaving her husband on top of the water tower, with the others following behind her. The cemetery was oddly serene as they crossed it, compared to the chaos and noise in the rest of the town. No trolls were here knocking over headstones or defiling burial sites. It was almost as if the trolls sensed that this a place that was not to be disturbed.

Beyond the graves, the struts of the water tower rose in a round, grassy little clearing. Groa dove at them as they entered the glade, her cackles echoing against the trees around the clearing.

"Awk!" Hulda honked, flapping out of Inga's arms and extending her neck to strike at the swooping witch.

Groa reached out to grab Hulda but withdrew her hand at the last moment, narrowly avoiding a beak snap. The witch veered away and zoomed back up. "I don't think so, you vicious creature. But when I do get my hand around your throat, you'll soon find yourself in a cooking pot with onions and carrots and a dash of fennel!"

"Awk!" Hulda protested at the retreating broomstick.

Far above them, Riley and Groschen looked over the top of the railing. "Santa!" Riley called down. "Be careful! The Troll King has—"

Before she could finish, Groschen clapped his green bean fingers over her mouth. "Well if it isn't good Saint Nicholas. You'll have to climb up here if you want to rescue the girl!"

"Skyrgámur." Nick snapped his fingers. "You're the best climber. See how fast you can get up there and bring Riley back down."

"But how will I get me mitts on her if the Troll King is holding her?" Skyrgámur asked.

"Leave that up to me," Nick lifted the Ulvehammer and gave Skyrgámur a wink. "I just need to practice my hammer throw. Now see how fast you can get up there."

"On it!" Skyrgámur leaped onto the rungs and ascended speedily.

"Mmpph!" Riley cried to Skyrgámur as she struggled to break free of Groschen's grip. "Mmpph mmpph!"

"Everybody back up and give me some room," Nick said to the others. When they'd stepped back, he held up his hand in an L and squinted through it a moment to judge the distance to the top of the water tower. "Hmm. Fifty yards, I'd say. Have to care not to hit Riley. Give the troll king's fringe a buzz. Should be doable."

"Just knock him down here, I'll take care of the rest," Inga said to Nick through gritted teeth.

Nick began his spin, the Ulvehammer humming as it picked up speed through the air.

"Oh, shit," Groschen muttered. He shouted over the side of the railing, "Groa, can you do something about that?"

"Mmm mmm mmm," Groa said from where she hovered nearby, eyeing Nick's powerful form. "I'd like to let him hammer me again. Maybe when all this is over?"

The Ulvehammer was positively whistling with speed. "Groa!" Groschen yelled.

"Fine, cousin. I'll knock him off course." She backed her broom up well above the bell of the water tower and began a nosedive.

As Skyrgámur scrambled up the ladder, he reached a place where he found he could no longer hold on to the rungs. "Ay! Lost me grip!" he squealed as he sailed through the air.

At that moment, Groa was speeding by. Skyrgámur flailed his arms and grabbed hold of the only thing he could reach, which was the tail end of Groa's broom. The shift in weight altered her trajectory, so instead of aiming at his body, her broom stick was aimed straight at the point where Nick was about to release the Ulvehammer.

"You fool!" she cried.

Eyes widening when he saw the coming impact, but unable to stop his momentum, Nick instead released the Ulvehammer a split second earlier. It just missed Groa and Skyrgámur and flew several feet short of its intended trolly target, instead hitting a support beam under the catwalk, which bent in half with a metallic crunch. The catwalk lurched to a forty-five degree angle toward the ground, and Riley and Groschen found themselves sliding toward the railing, which they grabbed with both hands before going over the edge. Freed of the troll king's hands, Riley screamed, her feet dangling into the air.

"Groa!" Groschen screeched. "That didn't make things better!"

"I'm a little busy, cousin!" Groa called back up, fending off Hulda, who had flapped onto the front of the broom as it'd sped by and now pecked wildly at Groa's arms and face, even while Skyrgámur still dangled from the back end. The broom jagged crazily through the air.

At the bottom of the water tower, Roscoe looked up one of the struts to where it met the tank above. "You know," he mused. "We don't need the ladder. I think I could climb this."

"Don't you dare!" Inga said. "Let the grown-ups handle this."

The damaged support emitted a groan and bent a bit more, sending a shudder through the catwalk. Riley screamed again.

"Sorry, Mom, the grown-ups can't do it, and somebody has to help that girl. It's up to me." He wrapped his arms and knees around the strut and shimmied up. "It's working!"

"Oh Roscoe, be careful!" Inga said, her voice quavering and one hand on her chest.

* * *

From his vantage hanging from the railing of the downward-jutting catwalk, Groschen observed the scene. Saint Nicholas was already recovering his hammer and would no doubt be making another throw shortly. Groa was zig-zagging through the sky with a maddened swan pecking her on one end and a squealing gnome hanging from her other. Two of his dumber trolls seemed to have turned against him and joined the band of his nemesis. His son was already a quarter of the way up the support strut and would arrive shortly to cause trouble, and Cindy Sue's great-granddaughter was climbing her way up the railing, hand over hand, to meet him. Worst of all, his enraged wife had her arms folded across her chest and was glowering up at him in a most perturbing way.

"Time to call out the big guns," Groschen muttered. Holding himself with one hand on the railing, he brought the fingers of his other hand to his lips and emitted an eardrum-rattling whistle. The sound pierced the night air, emanating from the water tower to reach the farthest corners of

Howburg. And wherever they heard it, the trolls stopped what mischief they were perpetrating, and started toward the source of the whistle.

Within moments, the entire army was on the move, trolls bounding, running, or marching to the water tower, leaving behind the befuddled but relieved townsfolk.

Chapter Twelve

The fastest and closest trolls passed through the cemetery and reached the water tower in short order. They screamed and shrieked as they ran, trampling timeworn graves, manicured lawns, and carefully tended landscaping alike, breaking the peace that had formerly reigned there.

When they emerged into the clearing, Nick and his trolls awaited them. Nick held his Ulvehammer, Stunker his thick oaken limb, and Grusom his hockey stick. The battle, once joined, did not end quickly, for as soon as Nick and his comrades had dispatched the first arrivals with rib-snapping, skull-splitting blows, a second wave was breaking over them, and soon they were surrounded by a mob of clamoring trolls three deep.

Bones splintered, hacked limbs spiraled away spurting blood, trolls screamed in sudden pain or, once felled, groaned in agony where they lay on the grass. Nick fought tirelessly, swinging the gore-drenched Ulvehammer against every foe within reach, each blow landing true. His example seemed to lend his companions courage as well, for Stunker and Grusom fought as they had never fought for the troll king: not only with ferocity, but with a grace and intelligence rarely seen in troll warriors. Indeed, one advantage the three had over the hordes of trolls coming against them was they way they worked together, rescuing one another from sticky situations, or joining to strike simultaneous blows against an overwhelmed opponent.

Yet, it was not clear that they would be victorious, for the stream of trolls was neverending: the majority of them huge brutes with protruding guts and heavy clubs, but interspersed with lanky snarlers with long, clawed limbs, and even others, serpentine and slithering their way into the action, nipping at Nick, Stunker, and Grusom from underneath with fanged mouths.

Overhead, Groa finally succeeded in snatching Hulda, gripping tightly onto the swan's gracile neck. "Ha, got you! I believe I'll turn you slowly on a spit over a low flame, drizzling you with lemon and Madeira to keep you juicy."

Hulda emitted a choked awk, her frenzied flapping and kicking to no avail in the witch's iron grasp.

"Ah, here we go," Skyrgámur said, scrambling his legs over the top of the wood and straddling the broomstick behind Groa. He put his vaseline-slicked hands over her eyes. "Guess who?"

"Take your hands off my face, you moron! I can't steer if I can't see, and this thing is overloaded as it is!" With one hand on the broomhandle and the other around the swan, Groa was reduced to shaking her head and wiggling her shoulders to try to evade the gnome's hands, each movement sending the broom lurching in a different direction. Wind rushed by them and the landscape shifted and blurred.

"That's not a very good guess," Skyrgámur said. "I'll give you another."

"I don't need another guess! You're one of those meddling little Yule Lads. Now get your goddamn hands off my face before I fry you with lightning and air mail you back to Reykjavik!"

"Warmer, but not quite right," Skyrgámur teased. "I'll give you one more guess, just because me heart's in the right place."

"Aaaiieee!" Groa screeched, as the broomstick took a sickening turn toward the ground at full speed.

Riley, moving hand over hand, had made her way up the railing of the listing catwalk halfway to where the strut met a support beam. She glanced to her right, where the troll king still dangled but seemed strangely serene considering his situation. She glanced to her left, where the handsome half-troll boy had climbed nearly to the top of the strut. The one place she did not look was down, where one hundred-fifty feet below, the ground waited should her grip falter.

"Hey, what's your name?" she called to the half-troll boy to distract herself from the danger.

"I'm Roscoe," he replied. "What's yours?"

"My name's Riley. Is that your mom down there, yelling at you to be careful?"

"Yeah, that's her," Roscoe said with an eye roll. "And that's my dad hanging on over there."

"Oh, your dad's the troll king?" Riley said.

"Yeah, that's right." Roscoe reached the top of the strut and passed his hands over to the grilling that made up the catwalk floor, now tilted down at an angle. He heaved himself up and thrust a hand forward, grabbing the metal holes with his fingers and pulling until he was able to lift a knee over the side, followed by his whole body. "Listen, I'm going to scoot down there and help lift you up, okay?"

"Fine with me," Riley said.

Roscoe inched his way down to where Riley hung from the railing. With one hand gripping the grillwork, he reached his other out and placed it around her left wrist.

"Listen, I have a hold of you," Roscoe said. "I want you to let go of the railing with that hand and grab my wrist. Then we'll do your other hand. Okay?"

Riley took a deep breath. "Sure."

"Whenever you're ready."

Riley released her left hand and took hold of Roscoe's wrist.

"All right, there's the first hand," Roscoe said. "Now let go with your other hand and grab my arm, and I'll pull you up here."

"Are you sure you're strong enough?" Riley asked.

Roscoe hesitated just a moment, but when he answered his voice was firm. "Yes, I'm strong enough."

Riley let go with her right hand, and for a brief moment a wave of vertigo passed through her, but then she clasped Roscoe's arm and it ended. Groaning with the effort, he hauled her up onto the grilled flooring and when she felt herself on the solid surface she collapsed, the breath she didn't even realize she'd been holding rushing out of her. Roscoe laid beside her, breathing heavily, sweat beading his temples.

"Thanks," Riley managed after she caught her breath. "You seem a lot nicer than your dad."

"Oh, he's not too bad," Roscoe said.

Riley gestured vaguely in the direction of the ruined town. "We'll have to agree to disagree on that one."

"For now, let's get you back down to the ground," Roscoe said, pushing himself up. "We'll have to go up to where the strut meets this catwalk, and then climb back down it."

Riley looked skeptically at the strut. "Are you sure?"

"Hey, I just climbed it all the way up here," Roscoe said. "Going down will be the easy part. I'll show you how."

"If you say so," Riley said, getting to her feet. She followed Roscoe as he clambered up the tilted surface.

At that moment, Groa's broomstick came looping up from somewhere below, headed right for the catwalk, with Groa screeching in terror at the impending collision.

"Abandon ship!" Skyrgámur squealed, leaping off the broomstick and landing on top of the railing next to where Groschen hung. Hulda took advantage of the distracted witch's loosened grip on her throat to squirm free and flap off into the darkness.

The broomstick hit the catwalk point forward, and the entire structure juddered, knocking Roscoe and Riley off their feet and sending them tumbling down. Roscoe managed to grab Riley's hand before she could slide all the way off into free air, but he couldn't stop his own momentum and they fell from the catwalk. Just before they plummeted, he caught a protruding steel beam and clutched it desperately, hanging on with one hand and holding Riley in his other, far, far above the earth.

Chapter Thirteen

"Oh my God, Roscoe, hang on!" Inga screamed. She could see the bottom of his tennis shoes slowly twisting and the pink fuzzy slippers of the girl who was desperately holding onto her son's arm.

"I am, Mom! But I don't know how much longer I can!"

Inga looked around frantically for someone who might be able to help. Nick and the two trolls were in the midst of a fray, with hacked off body parts flying through the air and arterial blood spraying everywhere. Hulda flapped around awk-ing in the air but what could a swan do? Groa had landed in a nearby tree and appeared to be passed out on a branch. Inga considered Skyrgámur, who was dancing along the railing singing "la, la, la" and stepping between Groschen's fingers. But she didn't think the little gnome had the strength to help here.

Finally, her attention settled on Groschen, hanging by both arms like a floppy greenbean pod dangling from a stem. Her eyes narrowed. Well, it didn't look like there was much choice in the matter.

"Groschen!" she yelled up to him.

"I'm a little busy at the moment, dear," he called back down.

"You are not, you're just hanging there doing nothing! And your son needs you to man up, right fucking now!"

"And just what is it you think I can do to help?" Groschen asked.

"You can do a single pull-up and raise yourself on that railing and then get over to where Roscoe and the girl are hanging on for their lives! And Skyrgámur's going to stop dancing and singing and get the hell out of your way to let you do it!"

"La, la...oh, right." Skyrgámur walked backwards several stops along the railing without looking.

"I suppose I could give it a try," Groschen called.

"You'd damn well better!" Inga screamed back. To herself, she added, "Please God, let him for once not fuck it up and actually do something right."

At the top of the water tower, Groschen pulled with his skinny, furry green arms and raised himself about three inches, then collapsed back into complete limpness, exhaling mightily.

"Ooh, I think me eye spied a muscle popping out," Skyrgámur said.

"Quiet, you," Groschen said.

"Help!" came Roscoe's voice. "I think I'm going to slip soon!"

"Keep holding on, son," Groschen called back in what he hoped was an encouraging way. *Your boy's depending on you,* he thought. *The heir to your kingdom, the future king of the trolls. You can do this, for him.*

He closed his eyes and tried again, his green face grimacing with the strain. Slowly, slowly, he lifted himself up to the railing bar. Finally, he hooked an elbow over the bar and hoisted himself onto it.

"All hail the mighty Troll King!" Skyrgámur said, making a deep bow.

Groschen ignored the gnome and came to all fours on the bar, walking along it with almost feline ease. When he reached the point where Roscoe and Riley hung from the steel beam, he made a graceful four-legged leap from the bar to the tilted catwalk.

"How to do this? How to do this?" he murmured to himself. He observed Riley's hand clasping Roscoe's, his grip the only thing keeping her from falling. "It'll have to be the girl first."

He latched onto the grillwork with the long toes of both his feet and the fingers of one hand and leaned out, head first, way over the edge, reaching as far as he could with his long green arm. "Riley, can you reach with your free hand and grab mine?"

Riley looked up at him with eyes widened in fear but didn't move. She seemed paralyzed from the terror of her situation.

"C'mon, honey, it'll be okay," Groschen reassured her. "Be a brave girl and reach up with your free hand. That's it, keep going."

Riley lifted her arm and her grip latched onto Groschen's. With a growl of exertion, Groschen used his legs and other arm to reverse climb up the catwalk until Riley could grasp the grilling. Once feeling herself on a solid, if angled, surface, Riley fell back and put a hand over her pounding heart.

Now for the boy, Groschen thought.

Taking advantage of the release of Riley's weight, Roscoe had managed to take hold of the steel beam with both hands. Still, he was too exhausted to lift himself any further.

Again anchoring himself with his feet, Groschen reached over and wrapped both his hands around Roscoe's forearms. "Got you, son. Go ahead and let go of the beam."

"I don't know if I can, Dad," Roscoe said. "We're too high up."

"C'mon, Roscoe. Do you trust me?"

"Well, yeah, but—"

"Then let go of the beam right now."

Roscoe did and Groschen hefted him up to the catwalk next to Riley.

"Okay, there we go. Both of you safe and sound," Groschen said.

"Not quite, Mr. Trollman," Riley said. "We still don't know how we're going to get back down."

"Hmm." Groschen eyed Groa's broom, lodged into a deformed section of catwalk metal. He made his way over and yanked it. When it didn't budge, he spit on his hands, rubbed them together, and took hold, giving the broomstick a mighty heave. It wrenched loose with a twisting of metal.

"Look out, folks, he's a real he-man!" Skyrgámur cried from where he still perched on the nearby railing.

"You know, there's no reason you can't go right back in the dungeon at Troll Castle," Groschen sniveled at him.

"Aye, but you have to catch me first!" Skyrgámur leapt onto a strut and slid down all the way to the ground.

"Yeah, because it would be so difficult to leave out some rancid milk product and simply wait for you to come along," Groschen muttered after him. He mounted the broom and gently kicked off with his toes, letting the broom drift up a few inches. He slowly floated his way back to Roscoe and Riley. "Hop on kids. I'll give you a ride down."

Riley eyed the broomstick suspiciously. "Is it safe?"

"Sure it is!" Roscoe said, climbing on behind his dad. "I've ridden Auntie Groa's broom lots of times."

He patted the stick behind him and Riley warily put a leg over it, wrapping her arms around Roscoe. She let out a little gasp when the broomstick levitated into the air. It soared up and around the back of the water tower and then looped to its front again, corkscrewing around the structure in descending spirals until finally landing on the grass in front of the waiting Inga.

"Oh, Roscoe, thank God!"

Inga gathered him up and this time didn't let go when he tried to wriggle free, until he finally cried out, "Moomm, stop!"

Inga set him down and he put his arms across his chest, giving her an aggrieved look.

"Well?" Inga said. "Aren't you going to introduce me to your friend?"

"Oh, right!" Instantly Roscoe's expression changed, and he put a hand on Riley's arm. "Mom, this is Riley. Riley, this is my mom, the queen of the trolls."

"You can just call me Mrs. Fryser," Inga said.

"How do you do?" Riley said politely, holding out her hand. Inga gave it a shake.

"Well?" Groschen said to Inga. "I got them down and no harm done."

"You certainly did." Inga stepped up to her husband and took his hands, putting them around her waist. She gave him a coy smile. "And you looked so strong when I saw you up there, lifting them without any thought of your own safety."

"Did I?" Groschen cleared his throat. "Well, I suppose I—"

Inga put a finger to his lips. "Maybe later when we get back to Troll Castle, I could stop by your chamber...."

"Really?" Groschen's face momentarily flashed confusion, but settled into a sort of quizzical happiness. "Well, yes. That would be lovely."

"But to do that, you'll have to give up your silly crusade against this town," Inga said.

"Consider it done," Groschen replied. "Shall we be on our way, then?"

"What about them?" Inga pointed to the ongoing fray, where Nick, Stunker, and Grusom continued to battle a never-ending stream of trolls in bone-shattering, bloodsoaked close combat. At that very moment, a blow from the Ulvehammer knocked a troll head clean from its shoulders, and the blood-spurting orb bounced almost to the feet of Groschen and Inga.

"Oh, right," Groschen said. He put his fingers to his lips and made a high-decibel whistle, albeit one that was not quite as eardrum-challenging as the earlier one. All the trolls stopped fighting instantly and looked to him. Nick glanced around in bewilderment at the sudden surcease in the action.

"Alright, boys," Groschen sniveled. "Time to head home."

Chapter Fourteen

Riley held Roscoe's hand as they sat next to Stunker and Grusom on the grass and watched the sun rise over the town of Howburg. Riley looked about to see what everybody was up to.

Roscoe's mom, Mrs. Fryser, stood next to the troll king as he assembled what was left of his army and lined them up. Santa had just returned with his sleigh and reindeer and was adjusting their harnesses. The beautiful elf-swan hunted for worms and grubs in the dewy grass, and Skyrgámur danced a jig among the corpses on the battlefield, singing an ode to creamy yogurt. Even the troll witch had awakened and come down from the tree, and was performing some sort of ritual to repair her broomstick.

Beyond the cemetery, the good people of Howburg had gone to work fixing all the damage to their town. Citizens were out replacing shingles on rooftops, clearing trash from streets, and nailing boards over broken windows. Nearly all the fires had been put out, and the Howburg Towing Company was doing a booming business in righting overturned vehicles and hauling away junked cars.

Finishing with his reindeer, Santa came and stood in front of them. Somehow he'd managed to wipe the gore away and his armor gleamed in the morning sun, his cape flapped, his long beard shone white.

"I saw what you two did last night," Santa said to Riley and Roscoe. "You were quite a courageous pair of children."

"Thank you," the two replied in unison.

"And I couldn't help but notice that you're quite a good climber, going up the strut of the water tower," Santa went on to Roscoe. "Where'd you learn to climb like that?"

"Oh, I like to climb the trees in Forbyr Forest," Roscoe said. "And sometimes I scale the walls around the castle, just for fun."

"I see," Santa said. "You're truly talented at it." He looked the boy in the eye. "In fact, I think you'd even be capable of climbing a sheer cliff wall. Say, one outside a workshop where an elf-swan is hidden?"

Roscoe's green-ish cheeks flushed red but he didn't speak.

"Is there anything you'd like to tell me?" Santa asked. His eyes twinkled and burned at the same time.

Riley squeezed Roscoe's hand to help him be brave.

"I...I did take the elf-swan," Roscoe said. "I didn't want to, but Dad said it had to be me. I climbed down the cliff and broke into your workshop. And I broke the window too, but that was an accident. And I left Skyrgámur's spoon so you would think it was him."

Hulda awk-ed her confirmation of the story and Skyrgámur's voice came floating from the battlefield, "So you're the one who had it!"

Roscoe's eyes welled with tears. "I know I won't get any Christmas presents in my stocking this year."

Santa put a hand on the boy's shoulder. "What you did was wrong, Roscoe, but you've told the truth about it, and that counts for a lot. And you've been brave all night, helping your friends and people in trouble. I don't think you need to worry about finding something in your stocking this year." He put his other hand on Riley's shoulder. "You either, Riley."

"Thank you, Santa," Riley said.

Turning to Stunker and Grusom, Santa went on. "In fact, if you two leave out stockings on Christmas Eve, I wouldn't be surprised if you found something nice in them come morning."

"Really?" Stunker said. "Even trolls get presents?"

"If they've been good, they can," Santa said.

The troll king had finished with his minions and he and Inga came walking along hand in hand. "And as for you—" Here Santa paused, looking the troll king in the eye. Groschen did not shrink from Santa's gaze, but Riley noticed his hands trembled. "I'll give you and your bride your Christmas present now."

"I can hardly imagine what you think would be appropriate for me," the troll king said.

"I'm not giving you what's appropriate for you," Santa said. "That would be a terrible thing. Though you did save the children in the end, so I'm inclined to be forgiving. Anyway, this is mostly a gift for Inga. Hold out your hand."

The troll king held it out. Santa pulled out a little leather pouch and took a pinch of a sparkling powder. He dropped it in the troll king's palm.

"You're giving me some elf dust?" the troll king said, amazed.

"Enough to get you and Inga to Miami and back," Santa said.

"Truly?" Inga asked. "Oh my, God, that would be marvelous. But wait, isn't Miami really hot?"

"Don't worry, they keep the air conditioning cranked everywhere you go," Santa said. "And I think you and Anya will be spending a lot of time shopping."

"Ooh, I can't wait!" Inga said.

"But I give you this on one condition." Nick closed the troll king's fingers around the precious grains.

"What's that?" the troll king said.

"You must accept Stunker and Grusom back into the troll ranks. And no more laundry for Stunker."

"I suppose so. Though who'll wash my socks?" He gave Inga a side glance. "You don't suppose, my dear, that—"

Mrs. Fryser stared him down hard. "You'd better not ask me what I think you're about to ask if you want to break your twelve-year losing streak."

The troll king swallowed and shut his mouth.

"What about me, Nick?" the troll witch asked, strolling up. "Do I get any elf dust for a trip to Miami?"

"Hell, no," Santa replied. "I'm keeping you as far from my wife as possible. Besides, you've already gotten your reward."

"Several times in one night, as I recall," the troll witch said, rubbing her hands up and down her hips.

Santa rolled his eyes. "So do you have enough enchantment left in the broom to get all the trolls back where they belong?"

"Yes, I think so," the troll witch said. She waved the tip of her broom in a circular motion and it created a glowing, humming rainbow. She drew the tip of the broom outward and the rainbow circle grew until it was large enough for a person or troll to pass through.

The troll king whistled, and the trolls started marching. He waved them through, one by one, finally snapping his fingers and pointing at Stunker and Grusom, who got up and followed the line.

"No laundry," Stunker said, shaking his head in disbelief. "My dream come true."

"What will you do with all your free time now?" Grusom asked him.

"I always want to try salsa dancing," Stunker said just before stepping into the portal.

Roscoe was next. He let go of Riley's hand and leaned over to give her a little kiss on the forehead before rising. "I'm sorry about what my dad did to your town."

"It's not your fault," Riley said. "You're nice. I know you're not the same."

"I hope I can come visit you sometime," he said. "Maybe when your town is all fixed up."

"Yes, I'd like that." Riley smiled at him. Roscoe smiled back and gave her a little wave before getting behind Grusom in the departure line.

Finally only the troll king, Inga, and the witch were left.

The troll king held out his hand and Santa gave it a shake.

"Now that we're such good friends," the troll king said. "I don't suppose I could bother you to lift the curse that prevents us from leaving Forbyr Forest."

"It's not my curse," Santa said. "I believe you'd have to ask Riley, the direct descendant of the one who laid the curse in the first place."

The troll king turned to Riley and gave her a slight bow. "You know, I did save your life there at the end, and—"

"No way," Riley said. "Thanks for saving me and all, but great-grandmother's curse is going nowhere."

"Very well, then," the troll king said, spinning on one green foot and hopping into the portal.

"I'm so excited!" Inga said. "We'll be down to visit as soon as I can get my bags packed."

"Travel to the Setai Hotel," Nick said. "We'll have a room reserved for you."

Inga leaned over and gave Nick a kiss on the cheek. "Thank you so much, Nick."

"My pleasure," Nick said as Inga stepped through. Only the troll witch was left.

"I don't suppose you'd come back up to my cottage for a visit sometime?" the witch asked.

Nick sighed. "Keep it moving, Groa."

"If you insist. But if you ever change your mind, you know where to find me." She fluttered her eyelashes and gave a coquettish wave before passing through the portal. Behind her, the portal shrank down to a soap bubble, momentarily shimmering rainbows in the morning sun. Then it popped and was gone.

"C'mon, Hulda, c'mon, Skyrgámur, let's get to the workshop," Santa said.

"Oh, goody!" Skyrgámur said, skipping over to the sleigh. Hulda flapped in the air with a happy awk and alighted on the sleigh's bench.

Before mounting the sleigh, Santa turned to Riley. "You'll send me your list, Riley?"

"Of course, Santa."

"Say hi to your mother for me," Santa said. "And if you continue being helpful around the house and brave and good-natured, I think you'll get most of what you ask for. But, you know, about the one thing on your list that you put every year... there are some things even magic can't perform."

"I know," Riley said. "But it's still what I wish for."

Santa nodded. "I understand. You're a good girl, Riley."

With that, Santa mounted the sleigh, took the reins, and gave them a shake. "On Donner, on Blitzen!" he yelled, and the reindeer began to run, picking up speed until the sleigh lifted off the earth and soared into the sky.

Riley watched until the sleigh disappeared in the distance before setting off through the cemetery. She stopped at a set of headstones set off a bit from the main path. One of the headstones read CINDY SUE, BELOVED MOTHER, GRANDMOTHER, AND GREAT GRANDMOTHER, AND LAYER OF THE CURSE THAT SAVED THE TOWN OF HOWBURG.

Riley patted the stone. "Thank you, Great-Grandmother," she whispered. "I miss you."

She moved to another stone and let her fingers drift across it. "And I miss you, too, Daddy. More than anyone."

And then she wiped an eye and continued on her way to her mother's house.

* * *

Hrodi was waiting in front of the workshop with Ipad in hand when Santa's sleigh came skidding to a stop among sprays of fresh powdery snow.

"What's the word, Hrodi?" Nick asked, dismounting with Hulda in his arms. A gnome in a yellow coat and a red cap bounded off beside him. Hrodi raised an eyebrow.

"Things are good here, Boss. We've been worried about you, though. Haven't heard from you since you left for Troll Castle on Tuesday night."

"Things have been interesting, I can say that for sure," Nick said.

"They must have been, for you to bring a Yule Lad home with you," Hrodi noted with a suspicious glance at the gnome.

"Ho ho! This is Skyrgámur, and he's become a good friend of mine."

Skyrgámur gave a bow to Hrodi. "Pleased to make your acquaintance, Mr. Elf-man. Skyrgámur be me name, yogurt gobbling be me game."

Hrodi cleared his throat. "Charmed, I'm sure. Shall we get down to business, Boss?"

"Yes, of course," Nick said. "Thanks for keeping me on track. We'll need to get Hulda back in her proper place, of course."

Hrodi snapped his fingers and a pair of elves carrying a white velvet pillow stepped out of the workshop. Nick held Hulda out and she settled on the cushion with a happy expression and a satisfied *awk*. The elves retreated back inside as quickly as they'd appeared.

Back at the sleigh, Blitzen stamped and snorted.

"Oh, of course," Nick said. "Donner and Blitzen need to be brushed down and fed. Put them on double hay rations and plenty of apples. The boys have had nothing but moss and grass tufts for almost three days."

Another snap and a team of elves appeared and began disconnecting the harnesses and brushing the reindeer. Donner gave a thankful shake of his sleigh bells.

"As for our guest, please have that spoon we found washed and returned to him," Nick said, gesturing to Skyrgámur. "And have the kitchen staff see if we don't have a big batch of yogurt. Mix some fresh raspberries in, as well. If Skyrgámur wishes to stay a night, give him a guest room."

Hrodi narrowed his eyes skeptically at Skyrgámur but gave another finger snap. An elf in an elegant blue coat, yellow trousers, and a red bow tie appeared, offering his arm. "Would you come with me, sir? I'll show you to your room."

Skyrgámur looped his arm through the attendant's, who led him into the workshop. "Now this is service. Much better than that dreadful Troll Castle dump. Thanks, Santa. I'll be leaving five stars on TripAdvisor!"

"Anything else, Boss?" Hrodi asked.

"Yes, one more thing," Nick said. "Send an echelon of elves to the town of Howburg. Our best engineers and builders. I'd say about fifty elves for two weeks should do it."

"Right now?" Hrodi dropped his Ipad to his side and stared in disbelief at Nick. "Boss, we'll have to delay building out the Comb-Her-Hair Mermaid Color Change Set® production line. I know I'm out of line here but I have to ask: what could be so important in Howburg?"

"The trolls went on a rampage there," Nick said. "Ripped apart the whole place. We have to help them rebuild."

"But Boss, it'll cost us ten thousand units of mermaids by December and—"

Nick held up a hand to cut off Hrodi's protestations. "Forget the fucking mermaids. This is more important. And send the bill to Troll Castle. Understood?"

"Got it, Boss," Hrodi said, already typing notes furiously into his Ipad. "Bill to Troll Castle."

"Okay, good. Now that we've got all that settled, what's the time in Miami?"

Hrodi checked his watch. "Mid-afternoon, about three-fifteen."

"Ah, I'll be just in time for the party then," Nick said. "I'm taking a shower. Have my armor and the Ulvehammer washed and polished, and a fresh pair of reindeer ready for my trip back. Hmm. Comet and Cupid could use the exercise."

"Comet and Cupid, you got it, Boss." Hrodi looked up at Nick over the rims of his eyeglasses. "Are you sure you're okay, Boss? You look a bit worn."

"Oh, I'm just stiff. It's nothing twenty minutes under some steaming hot water won't fix." Nick stretched his arms back until his shoulders popped. "I'll tell you the whole sordid story sometime, Hrodi. But right now, I'm under the gun. If I'm not back at the hotel in time for Anya's birthday party tonight, I will be royally fucked."

"Got it, Boss." Another snap and a team of elves appeared and started removing Nick's armor. "I've already got the water heating, and the reindeer are being harnessed as we speak. Let's see if we can keep you off the missus's naughty list."

Epilogue

Anya checked her white gold Baignoire Cartier watch. "Six forty-five," she muttered to herself. "He has fifteen minutes. Ah, who am I kidding? He's not going to make it."

She glanced at the guests beginning to gather on the buttery leather sofas on the islands in the indoor reflecting pool in the hotel's open-walled party suite. The women wore colorful, clingy silk dresses and the men sported pastel suits over open-necked floral print shirts. They held crystal flutes of champagne and chatted in subdued tones, broken by little bursts of chittering women's laughter. All were beautiful and stylish, but none so much as Anya herself in her short black evening dress and simple pearl necklace and pearl earrings.

"Shit." Anya grabbed a champagne flute from a passing waiter and took a long sip. "And I really did want to wear my new lingerie for him."

From behind her came a squealing "Anya? Is that you?"

It was a voice she hadn't heard in decades. "It can't be." Anya spun and gazed in disbelief at the blonde woman rushing toward her, wearing an exquisite pale blue dress with lace sleeves and spangled with dark blue snowflake motifs. "Inga! Is it really you?"

The two women embraced each other. "Yes, it is! Oh, Anya, I finally made it for a visit!"

"Oh my God!" Anya held Inga's shoulders at arm-length. "Look at you! You look great!"

"Thank you. You do, too." Inga blushed, then gestured at the impossibly slender, green-whiskered man beside her in a lime seersucker suit, oversized tourist sunglasses, and a floppy straw hat. "You remember Groschen, of course?"

"Oh, of course!" Anya ignored Groschen's proffered hand and instead hugged him as well. "I haven't seen either of you since the wedding!"

"Yes, it's been far too long," Groschen sniveled. "I'm usually so busy, but I finally found some time for us to break free for a few days."

A strong, familiar hand landed on Anya's shoulder and she relaxed as it gave her a squeeze. "Ho ho," came a deep rumbling voice from behind her. "Spend as much time here as you like, Groschen. It's a gift to the two of you from Anya and me. Perhaps a belated wedding present, if you will."

"Nick!" Anya turned and sank in as her husband took her in his arms. "You're back!"

"Of course. Did you doubt I would be?" Nick kissed her tenderly on the cheeks, then brushed her lips with his.

"Well, you sure cut it close," Anya pointed out.

"I know it, baby," Nick said in a low tone. "I'll tell you the whole story later. Including a part I have to admit that you may not like."

Anya took in Nick's wrinkled forehead and apprehensive eyes and had an inkling of what his admission might be. She put a hand on his chest. "Now, Nick. You remember our rule: 'If it happens on the sleigh, that's where it will stay.'"

"I'm so glad to hear you say that," Nick said. "I've been worried sick how you would take it."

"Right now," Anya said. "All I want to do is enjoy my birthday party." She leaned in and whispered in his ear. "And later tonight, after everyone goes home, I want nothing more than to wear my special new outfit for you, and let you unwrap this present."

*And now let's leave Santa and Mrs. Claus
to their private moment
but don't be sad, dear reader,
for they'll be back before you know it.*

*Yes, they'll be back next year
with a big, brand new adventure.
So be good this year, and on Christmas Eve,
you'll be one who Santa will remember.*

I hope you enjoyed this inaugural entry in the Hard Santa series! Santa will be back for future Christmas stories. Thanks for reading! Nick.

I'd like to thank all the people who helped me in the writing and production of this book, especially Steve Moriarty, as well as the members of the Writers of Chantilly, who did so much to improve this book with their comments and suggestions!